ONE OCTOBER . . .
HERE YOU GO, ANDREW. YOU'VE EARNED IT.

MY OWN COSTUME?!
EACH YEAR, I GIVE ONE TO THE MOST HEROIC BOY IN THE WORLD . . . AND YOU'RE IT! HAPPY HALLOWEEN!
. . . HALLOWEEN . . .

. . . HALLOWEEN . . .

IT'S HALLOWEEN!

THUMP! THUMP! THUMP!

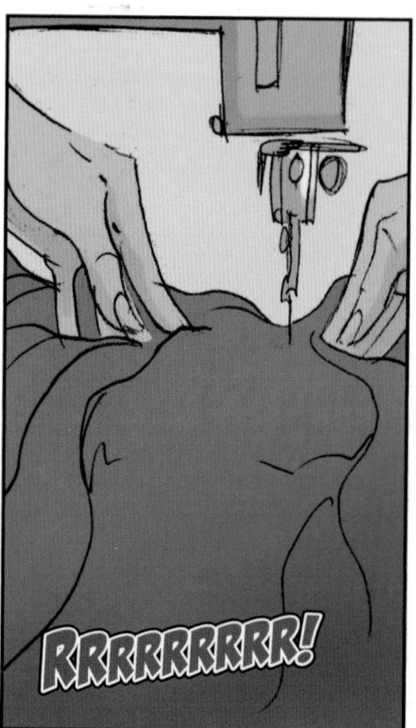
RRRRRRRRR!

BRUSHA!
BRUSHA!

DIGADIGADIGADIGADIGA!

HALLOWEEN, HALLOWEEN, **HALLOWEEN!**

MOM! DID YOU GET THE **DEFENDER** COSTUME?
GOOD MORNING, ANDREW!

OH, SWEETIE . . . I WENT TO EVERY SINGLE STORE LAST NIGHT AND THEY WERE ALL SOLD OUT.
YOU DIDN'T GET IT?!

WHAT AM I GONNA WEAR AT SCHOOL?!

DON'T WORRY. . .

I MADE YOU A DEFENDER COSTUME INSTEAD!

YOU MADE ONE?
BUT, UH, IT DOESN'T LOOK, UM . . .

I EVEN DUG UP MY GRANDPA'S WORLD WAR II GOGGLES AND SOME LONG UNDERWEAR!
NOW YOU'LL LOOK JUST LIKE DEFENDER!

THANKS, MOM!
WONDER IF IT'S TOO LATE TO PRETEND I'M SICK?

LOOK AT ALL THESE COOL DEFENDER AND MAGUS COSTUMES! MAYBE NOBODY WILL NOTICE MINE.
MAYBE I CAN HIDE IN THE TEACHERS' LOUNGE ALL DAY. . . .

NICE COSTUME, ANDREW! DID YOUR MOMMY MAKE IT FOR YOU?
SIGH
. . . OUT OF YOUR DAD'S UNDERWEAR?!

AT RECESS.
NOTHING CAN BOTHER ME DURING WALLBALL!
HEY, LOOK!

IT'S THE REAL DEFENDER VERSUS THE HOMEMADE DEFENDER!

HEY, GARETH, WHY DON'T YOU—

PUNG!

HAW, HAW! HIS SUPER-POWERED PAJAMAS DIDN'T PROTECT HIM!

YOU OK?
THAT'S A TOTAL DO-OVER!

NEVER MIND. RECESS IS ALMOST OVER ANYWAY. . . .

IF I HAD REAL POWERS, I'D KICK GARETH TO THE MOON!
EVERY NIGHT I'D LOOK AT THE BIG, FAT CRATER HE MADE AND LAUGH!

AFTER SCHOOL.

I WAS GONNA GO TO A *PARTY!* WHY CAN'T ANDREW GO TRICK-OR-TREATING ALONE?!
BECAUSE I HAVE TO GO TO ***WORK!*** AND HE'S ONLY ***NINE.*** IT ISN'T ***SAFE!***

I'M NOT A ***BABY,*** MOM! I'M BIG ENOUGH TO GO BY ***MYSELF!***
SEE?!

TOMMY, YOU'RE TAKING HIM TRICK-OR-TREATING — ***END*** OF DISCUSSION!

WHAM!
I ***HATE*** HALLOWEEN!

I'M ***NOT*** HOLDING YOUR HAND! AND I GET ***HALF*** YOUR CANDY!

VROOOOOOM!

DUDE! GO BACK!

RRRRRRTT!

HEY, TOMMY, WE'RE GOIN' TO THE PARTY! HOP IN!

UNLESS YOU HAVE TO BABYSIT. HA, HA!

I TOOK YOU TRICK-OR-TREATING, THEN WE WATCHED MOVIES. IF YOU TELL MOM ANYTHING ELSE . . .
YOU'LL HAVE TO DRINK YOUR CANDY THROUGH A STRAW!
FINE WITH ME!

I HOPE YOU HOOLIGANS GET ARRESTED!

FREEEEEEDOOOOOOM!
VROOOOM!

FINALLY, I CAN HAVE SOME FUN!

MUCH LATER.
GOOD HAUL TONIGHT! IF I HEAD HOME NOW, I MIGHT STILL CATCH THE DEFENDER HALLOWEEN SPECIAL ON TV!

UH-OH . . .
WIMP TAX! COST IS ONE BAG OF CANDY!
NO FAIR! YOU CAN'T HAVE MY CANDY — I EARNED IT! GET YOUR OWN CANDY, GARETH!

THE WHINER TAX IS A MOUTHFUL OF MY FIST!
HERE, HAVE ALL MY CANDY! HOPE YOU LIKE IT!

WHAT A JERK! I'D LIKE TO KNOCK GARETH AROUND — SEE HOW HE FEELS!

HMM. WHAT WOULD DEFENDER DO?

ALL RIGHT, WHO'S NEXT? WE ONLY GOT ROOM FOR A FEW MORE BAGS!
WE SHOULD MAKE THOSE **DWEEBS** CARRY 'EM FOR US!

HEY, LET'S MAKE THOSE **NERDS** CARRY OUR BAGS FOR US!
HA! THAT'S A **GREAT** IDEA!

TRICK OR TREAT, CHUMPS!
HUH?

YESSSSS! I GOT IT! HA-HA!
WHAP!
THUD!

DUDE . . . ?

WHOA! I'M SWINGING BACK! GOTTA STOP MYSELF!

COME TO PAPA, NERD!

HUNFF!
SMACK!

OOF!

HEY, LOOKIT! I GOT HIS CANDY, TOO!

JUST FOR THAT, YOU OWE ME YOUR LUNCH EVERY DAY THIS WEEK!
YOUR MOM HAD BETTER MAKE SOMETHING I **LIKE** — NO **VEGGIES!**

WHEN AM I GONNA **LEARN?** I'LL NEVER BE **HALF** THE HERO DEFENDER IS. . . .

HERE'S ALL THE CANDY I HAVE LEFT.
THANKS FOR TRYING, "DEFENDER."

THAT KID HAD A WEIRD COSTUME.

I **HATE** HALLOWEEN.
BARK! BARK! BARK!

BEING A HERO IS **HARD WORK.** AT LEAST MY COSTUME HELD UP!

JUST WAIT TILL NEXT YEAR, GARETH. . . .

MOST HEROIC BOY . . . ZZZZZ!

SNORT!

ZZZZ

SMASH

TRIAL BY FIRE

WRITTEN BY CHRIS A. BOLTON

ART BY KYLE BOLTON

COLORS BY CHRISTINA MACKIN AND SARAH BARRIE FENTON

 FIRST U.S. PAPERBACK EDITION 2018. LIBRARY OF CONGRESS CATALOG CARD NUMBER 2012947720. ISBN 978-0-7636-5596-9 (HARDCOVER). ISBN 978-0-7636-5406-1 (PAPERBACK). THIS BOOK WAS TYPESET IN ANIME ACE AND BADABOOM. THE ILLUSTRATIONS WERE DONE IN PENCIL AND COLORED DIGITALLY. CANDLEWICK PRESS, 99 DOVER STREET, SOMERVILLE, MASSACHUSETTS 02144. VISIT US AT WWW.CANDLEWICK.COM. PRINTED IN HESHAN, GUANGDONG, CHINA. 18 19 20 21 22 23 LEO 10 9 8 7 6 5 4 3 2 1

CANDLEWICK PRESS

FOR MOM
C. A. B.

FOR MOM AND JAMIE
K. B.

SIX MONTHS LATER . . .

C'MON, YOU PUNKS! LET'S WRAP THIS UP BEFORE LUNCH!

I MIGHT EVEN WORK UP AN APPETITE!

ALTHOUGH I *DOUBT* IT!

WHAP!
THUD!

NOT IF *THIS* IS THE BEST YOU CAN DO.

BACK OFF!

PAJAMA PARTY'S **OVER,** CREEPS!

IF YOU MESS WITH **DEFENDER,** YOU'VE GOTTA DEAL WITH HIS **SIDEKICK,** TOO!
THANKS FOR THE HAND, **SPARROWHAWK!** NOW SHOW 'EM WHAT I TAUGHT YOU!

THWACK!
BAM!
WHUD!
BIFF!!

NICE JOB, SPARROWHAWK! I COULDN'T HAVE DONE IT WITHOUT YOU, CHUM!
WELL, I LEARNED FROM THE BEST! NOW LET'S GO FIND THE MAGUS!

WE'LL TAKE THE FIGHT TO HIS—

LOOK OUT!

WHEN DID THE BOSTON TEA PARTY TAKE PLACE?

UH . . .
WHAT?

MR. RYAN! IF YOU CAN'T PAY ATTENTION IN *CLASS,* YOU CAN STAY IN AND PAY ATTENTION DURING *RECESS!* GOT IT?
Y-Y-YES, MR. LOFTON!

CAN *ANYONE* HELP OUT MR. RYAN?
NICE GOING, GENIUS.
LIKE *YOU* KNEW THE ANSWER, GARETH!
THE ANSWER IS DECEMBER 16, 1773!

IF YOU MISS RECESS, WE WON'T GET TO KICK YOUR BUTT AT WALLBALL!
THAT'S THE BEST PART OF MY DAY!
TSK TSK! THAT'D BE A SHAME. . . .

AT RECESS.
I GOT IT! I GOT IT! I—

MISSED IT!
SMOOTH MOVE, EX-LAX!

SOMEDAY I'M GONNA SMASH THAT BALL INTO GARETH'S FACE! THEN HE'LL BE THE ONE WHO GETS LAUGHED AT!

BACK IN CLASS.
WHY DO I HAVE TO FIGURE OUT HOW MANY TIMES 25 GOES INTO 450?! WHO CARES? I HATE DIVISION!

PTUI!
THWACK!

WHAT HIT ME? SOMETHING SOFT... FEELS SORT OF LIKE...

GUM?
BWA-HA-HA!

THE WAREHOUSE DISTRICT.
HE'S LATE.

THE MEN ARE IN POSITION, CAPTAIN.
HE'S NEVER LATE.

CAPTAIN RAMSEY, SIR, WE HAVE TO MOVE NOW! IF WE WAIT ANY LONGER . . .

ALL UNITS BE ADVISED— DEFENDER IS ON SCENE!

DEFENDER! OVER HERE!
LONG MEETING WITH YOUR PUBLICIST?
SMILE FOR THE CAMERAS, OLD MAN.

WE'VE GOT A MAN INSIDE WHO SAYS THE MAGUS IS HOLED UP IN THIS ROOM HERE, WITH A COUPLE DOZEN OF HIS MINIONS.
I WON'T EVEN BREAK A SWEAT!

HIS CONTROL ROOM IS HERE—BUT IT'S SURROUNDED BY ARMED GUARDS AND BOOBY TRAPS!

SO BE CAREFUL THIS TIME!
JUST HAVE A LOT OF HANDCUFFS READY!

. . . A SPECIAL BULLETIN FROM ACTION FIVE NEWS!
STUPID GARETH BREEDLOVE! I'D LOVE TO STUFF A FISTFUL OF GUM IN HIS HAIR!

COMING TO YOU LIVE FROM THE WAREHOUSE DISTRICT, WHERE DEFENDER IS ENTERING A BUILDING . . .
WHAT? DEFENDER, LIVE?!

. . . RUMORED TO BE THE HIDEOUT OF THE EVIL MASTERMIND CALLED THE MAGUS.
LIVE

THE MAGUS IS CONSIDERED THE GREATEST AND DEADLIEST—
—CHICKEN YOU'VE EVER TASTED! FIRST WE TENDERIZE THE MEAT, THEN—
CLICK!

HEY! CHANGE IT BACK, TOMMY! I WAS WATCHING THAT!
I HAVE THE REMOTE, AND I WANT TO WATCH COOKING.

YOU DON'T KNOW HOW TO COOK!
MM-MM! I LOVE COOKING! LOVE IT ALL THE TIME!
GIMME THE REMOTE!

HEY, ANDREW, WHO MAIMED THE OLD GRAY MARE?
NOOOOO!

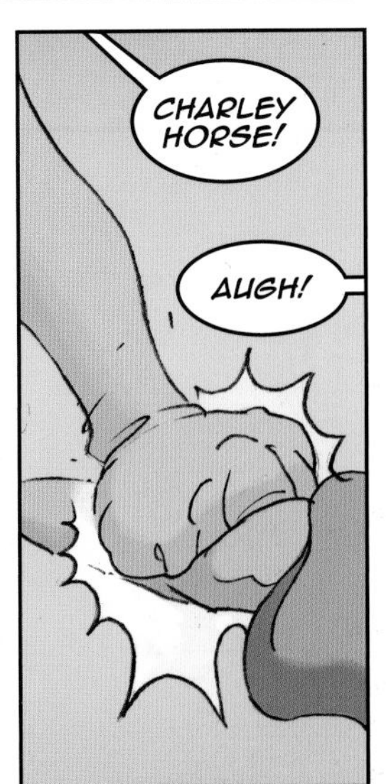
CHARLEY HORSE!
AUGH!

STUPID JERK!
AND IF YOU TELL ON ME, I'LL POUND YOUR OTHER ARM, TOO!

IF I WAS DEFENDER, I'D SNATCH THAT REMOTE RIGHT OUT OF TOMMY'S HANDS AND PUNCH HIM THROUGH THE WALL!
YEAH, RIGHT. LIKE THAT COULD EVER HAPPEN.

WHUP! WHUP! WHUP! WHUP! WHUP!
WISH I COULD SEE DEFENDER CATCH THE MAGUS!

WHUP! WHUP! WHUP! WHUP! WHUP!
IF I ONLY KNEW WHERE THAT HIDEOUT WAS, I COULD JUMP ON MY BIKE AND . . .

WHUP WHUP WHUP WHUP WHUP WHUP WHUP WHUP WHUP

I'LL FINALLY GET TO SEE DEFENDER . . . IN PERSON!

BACK AT THE WAREHOUSE.
WHERE ARE THE LIGHTS IN THIS PLACE?
BETTER TREAD CAREFULLY. THE MAGUS IS SURE TO HAVE SET A TRAP. . . .

AH, THERE'S THE SWITCH! NOW, LET'S SEE WHAT KIND OF —

CLICK!
OH, MAMA!

YOU WANNA DANCE, BOYS? I'LL LEAD!
HOW MANY TIMES IS THE MAGUS GONNA TRY THIS . . .

BEFORE HE RUNS OUT OF MINIONS?
CRASH!

FWIP!

CRACK!
WHATEVER THE MAGUS IS PAYING YOU PEOPLE . . .

JUST CAN'T BE WORTH THIS ABUSE!

POW!

AND THAT LEAVES . . . ONLY YOU. I HIGHLY RECOMMEND YOU SURRENDER.

YAAAHHHH!
TELL YOUR BOSS I'M VERY DISAPPOINTED. I EXPECTED A MUCH BETTER TRAP AFTER ALL THESE YEARS!
FWIP!
FWIP!
FWIP!
FWIP!
BUDA BUDA BUDA BUDA BUDA!

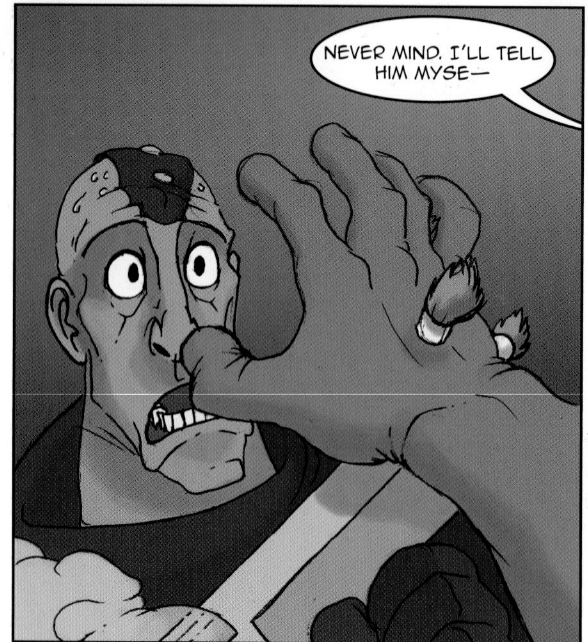
NEVER MIND. I'LL TELL HIM MYSE—

WHEW!
WHUMP!

NOT FAR AWAY.
MAYBE DEFENDER WILL MAKE ME HIS PARTNER!
HE'LL SEE WHAT I CAN DO—AND THEN I'LL SHOW EVERYONE!
WELL, WELL! IF IT ISN'T OL' BUBBLE HEAD!

WHERE ARE YOU GOING . . . ANDREW CRY-AN?
NONE OF YOUR BUSINESS!
SCREEE!

IF YOU WANNA GET PAST US, YOU GOTTA PAY THE TOLL!

ONE DOLLAR, WIMP!

HEY! GET BACK HERE!
WHY DON'T YOU JUST SEND ME THE BILL?

OF ALL THE TIMES TO RUN INTO GARETH! I'VE GOTTA LOSE HIM . . . BUT HOW?!

OH, MAN . . . THIS IS SO CRAZY!

JUST HOPE I CAN MAKE IT!

YOU DIDN'T ACTUALLY THINK YOU'D GET AWAY, DIDJA?
YOU'RE MINE NOW, WIMP!

WHOOOOO-HAAAA!

PLEASE, PLEASE, PLEASE DON'T KILL ME. . . .
GUH?

I WANT TO LIVE!
GAAAAHH!

OW!
OOF!
OUCH!

I **MUST** BE ALIVE 'CAUSE I **HURT** ALL OVER!

AUGH! MY **WRIST!** HOPE I DIDN'T **BREAK** IT . . .

NOWHERE TO RUN NOW, PUNK! OHHH, I'M REALLY GONNA ENJOY THIS . . .

INSIDE THE WAREHOUSE.
DEFENDER?
WAKEY, WAKEY!

UNH . . . WHAT? WHERE . . . ?

IT WOULD BE SO RUDE OF YOU TO SLEEP THROUGH MY MOMENT OF GLORY!

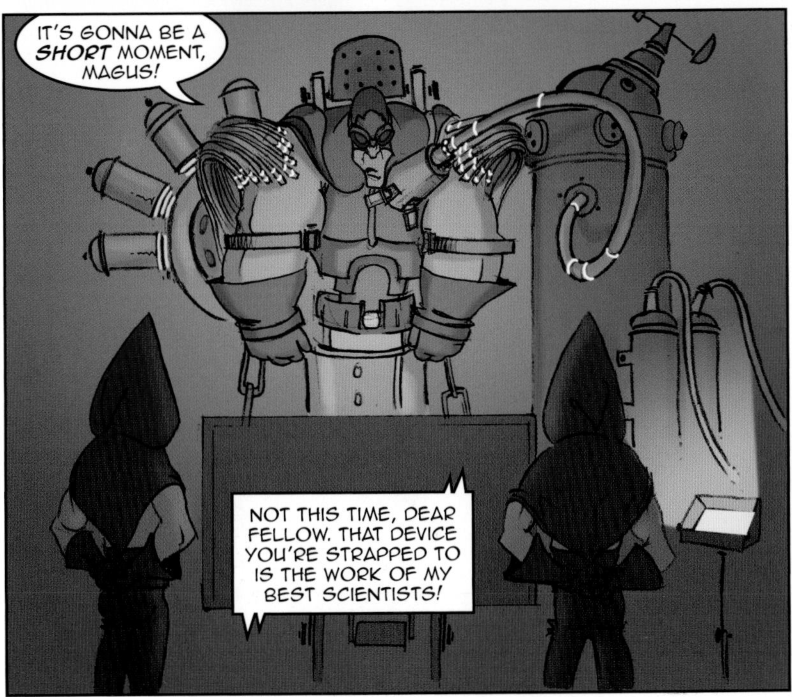
IT'S GONNA BE A SHORT MOMENT, MAGUS!
NOT THIS TIME, DEAR FELLOW. THAT DEVICE YOU'RE STRAPPED TO IS THE WORK OF MY BEST SCIENTISTS!

IT WILL DRAIN YOUR POWERS AND LEAVE YOU AN EMPTY SHELL . . .
LIKE A DISCARDED WRAPPER FLUNG IN THE TRASH!

I'VE BEEN SO LOOKING FORWARD TO HARNESSING YOUR POWERS FOR MYSELF! FAREWELL, OLD FRIEND!

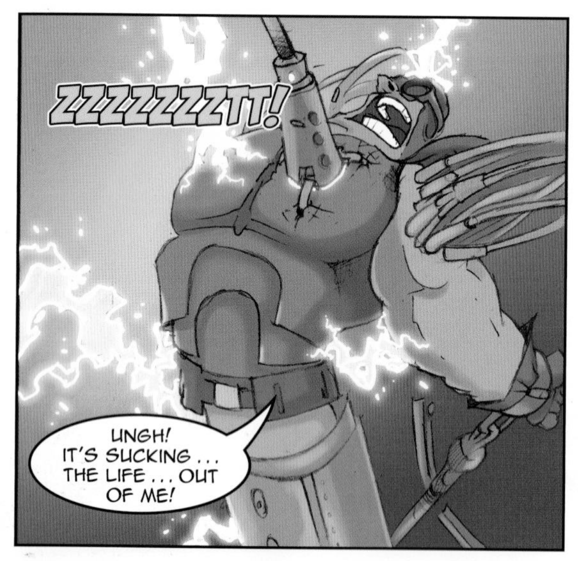
ZZZZZZZZTT!
UNGH! IT'S SUCKING . . . THE LIFE . . . OUT OF ME!

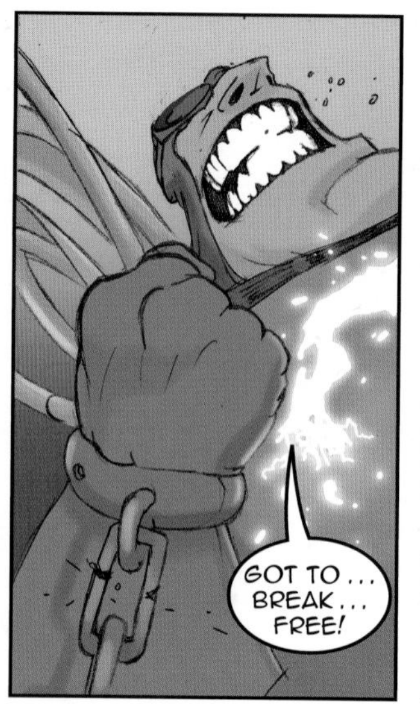
GOT TO . . . BREAK . . . FREE!

SNICK!

NOW, I'LL JUST PULL THIS THING OFF . . .

HA! TOO EASY—

KA-BOOM!!!

THAT CAN'T BE GOOD.

FOOM!

NEARBY.
I'M W-WARNING YOU GUYS. IF YOU GET ME C-CORNERED, I'M LIKE A C-CAGED ANIMAL!
THE FEE FOR RUNNING IS GETTIN' YOUR BUTT KICKED!

HOLY—!

I M-MEAN IT! S-S-STAY **BACK!**

RUN FOR YOUR LIVES!

BOOM!!

WHUNF!

INSIDE THE WAREHOUSE.
CRACK!

CLEAR!
ALL CLEAR!
ROOM IS SECURE!

ANY SIGN OF DEFENDER? OR THE MAGUS? OR ***ANYONE?***
OVER HERE!

THIS COULD BE AN ESCAPE ROUTE . . . IF ANYONE MADE IT OUT ALIVE. . . .

THERE'S ***MORE*** IN THE NEXT ROOM!

THIS ROOM LOOKS LIKE THE ORIGIN OF THE EXPLOSION.
CALL FORENSICS IN FOR A FULL SWEEP. I WANNA KNOW IF DEFENDER MADE IT OUT ALIVE!

ARE YOU KIDDIN'? THAT GUY COULD SURVIVE AN ATOM BOMB STRAPPED TO HIS BACK! OF ***COURSE*** HE MADE IT OUT—
SIR!

WE FOUND SOMETHING . . .

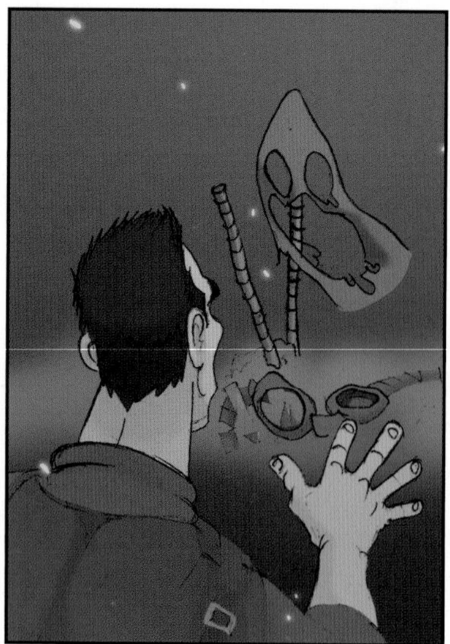

TEAR THIS PLACE APART! IF THERE'S A BODY, I WANT IT FOUND!

BACK AT THE CONSTRUCTION SITE.

UNH . . .

FEELS LIKE I TOOK A NAP FOR TEN YEARS!
WHAT IN THE WORLD HIT ME?

THAT'S WEIRD . . . MY **WRIST** . . . IT DOESN'T HURT ANYMORE!

WELL, WELL, WELL!

YOU'RE STILL ALIVE! THAT MEANS WE GET TO POUND YOU!
SHOULD'A PAID THE TOLL, WIMP!

MAYBE YOU MISSED IT, BUT I JUST GOT ZAPPED BY SOME KINDA SPACE RAY! CAN WE FINISH THIS LATER?

GET HIM!

WHAT THE . . . ?
SINCE WHEN CAN HE RUN SO FAST?!

MAN, THIS FEELS
GOOD! I'M NOT EVEN
WINDED—I COULD
RUN ALL DAY!

THIS IS TOO
MUCH WORK! PANT!
LET'S GO PICK ON
SOMEONE ELSE!
WHOA! I'M TOO
FAST FOR THEM!
THAT'S WEIRD . . .

YIKES!

GOING
TOO FAST . . . !

CAN'T STOP . . .

HOLY MONKEY!

YAAAAAHHH!

PARDON ME!
SORRY ABOUT THIS!

AM I REALLY FLYING?

THIS IS BEYOND WEIRD!

WHOOOOOAH!
I'M ALIVE!

I DON'T KNOW HOW...
AND I DON'T CARE! I'M
ACTUALLY FLYING!

WAA-HAAAAAA!

WHOA, BOY!
I'M UP WAAAY
TOO HIGH!

BETTER COME DOWN
OR I'M GONNA SPEW!

GOTTA DO IT JUST LIKE IN
THE "DEFENDER" VIDEO GAME!
SLOW DOWN . . . COME IN LOW . . .
BUT NOT TOO LOW!
STEADY . . .
EASY DOES IT . . .
ALMOST THERE!
SAL'S SEAFOOD
SAL'S
SAL'S

YIPES!
TOO FAST!

I DON'T
WANNA DIE!

CRASH!

UGH, MY
TUMMY . . .

BLURGH!

BOY, THAT TRUCK IS WRECKED! BUT THE ONLY PAIN I HAVE IS IN MY STOMACH . . .

NONE OF THIS MAKES ANY SENSE. UNLESS . . . MAYBE I DIED IN THAT BLAST AND NOW I'M A GHOST!

WOW! LOOK AT THAT HOLE! I CAN'T BELIEVE I SURVIVED THAT.

IF I'M A GHOST, I WOULDN'T HAVE CRASHED INTO THE TRUCK . . . AND GARETH AND HIS GOONS WOULDN'T HAVE SEEN ME . . . RIGHT?

THIS IS THE WEIRDEST DAY EVER! I'M GONNA GO TO BED.

WHEN I WAKE UP TOMORROW, EVERYTHING WILL BE BACK TO . . .

NORMAL?
ANDREW, YOU'RE *BACK!*
AGAIN, IN TONIGHT'S TOP STORY, . . .

MOM? W-WHAT'S WRONG?
OH, SWEETIE, I'M *SO* SORRY . . .

IT'S ALL OVER THE NEWS.

AFTER A THOROUGH INVESTIGATION, WE HAVE CONCLUDED THAT THE SUPERHERO CALLED DEFENDER . . .
IS *OFFICIALLY DEAD.*

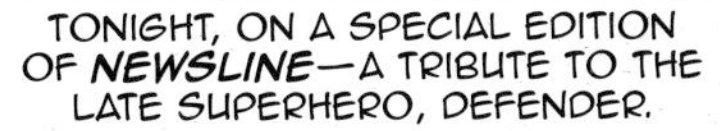
TONIGHT, ON A SPECIAL EDITION OF NEWSLINE—A TRIBUTE TO THE LATE SUPERHERO, DEFENDER.

HE FIRST APPEARED FIFTEEN YEARS AGO IN AMATEUR FOOTAGE THAT BECAME A GLOBAL SENSATION. . . .

WITH SUPERHUMAN STRENGTH AND THE ABILITY TO FLY, DEFENDER HAD POWERS FAR GREATER THAN ANY OTHER COSTUMED HERO.

ALTHOUGH HIS TRUE IDENTITY REMAINS A SECRET EVEN IN DEATH, DEFENDER REVEALED HIMSELF TO THE WORLD IN THIS HISTORIC TV INTERVIEW.
FOR THE GOOD OF EVERYONE, I CAN'T DISCUSS HOW I GOT THESE POWERS. BUT TRUST ME, THEY'RE REAL—AND AWESOME! AND I'LL USE THEM TO FIGHT CRIME UNTIL MY LAST BREATH.

SADLY PROPHETIC WORDS. DEFENDER MANIA SWEPT THE WORLD, INSPIRING MANY COPYCATS—THOUGH NONE OF THEM LASTED LONG. STILL, HE WAS NOT WITHOUT CONTROVERSY. . . .

LAW-ENFORCEMENT OFFICIALS, INCLUDING SEATOWN POLICE CAPTAIN DOUGLAS RAMSEY, HAVE OBJECTED TO HIS CRIME-FIGHTING ESCAPADES.
DEFENDER'S ARROGANT GRANDSTANDING INTERFERES WITH REAL COPS DOING THEIR JOBS. WE'D ALL BE A LOT SAFER IF HE HUNG UP HIS CAPE!

NONETHELESS, HE REMAINS A ROLE MODEL TO MILLIONS OF CHILDREN AND ADULTS ALL OVER THE WORLD. DEFENDER'S DEATH LEAVES MANY UNANSWERED QUESTIONS. . . .

WHO WAS HE? WHO COULD REPLACE HIM? AND IS ANYONE ELSE POWERFUL ENOUGH TO DEFEAT A CRIMINAL MASTERMIND LIKE THE MAGUS?

LATER THAT WEEK.
WHAT MAKES A HERO?
IS IT SOMEONE WHO RISKS HIS LIFE SO THAT OTHERS MAY LIVE IN PEACE?

IS IT SOMEONE WHO SACRIFICES HIS OWN WANTS FOR THE NEEDS OF THE WEAK AND HELPLESS?

DEFENDER WAS BOTH OF THESE . . . AND MORE. HE WAS THE GREATEST HERO OUR WORLD HAS EVER KNOWN.
AND NOW . . . HE IS GONE.

BUT HIS MEMORY WILL LIVE ON. AND WE PAY TRIBUTE TO HIS LEGACY BY TRYING TO LIVE OUR LIVES THE BEST WAY WE CAN.
REMEMBER

THAT'S WHAT HE WOULD HAVE WANTED . . .

DEFENDER GOT RID OF THE DRUG DEALERS IN FRONT OF MY HOUSE. I FELT SAFE LETTING MY SON PLAY ON OUR OWN STOOP. WHO'S GOING TO KEEP US SAFE ***NOW?***
REMEMBER

SORRY I'M LATE! MY MEETING RAN LONG. DID I MISS MUCH?
ONLY THE EULOGY. NOW PEOPLE ARE SHARING THEIR MEMORIES.

HOW'S HE DOING, HELEN?
JUST ***ASK*** HIM, THOMAS.

I WROTE A BLOG MAKING FUN OF HIS COSTUME. THEN SOME PUNKS STOLE MY MOST VALUABLE COMICS, AND DEFENDER CAUGHT THEM.
I NEVER GOT TO APOLOGIZE, OR THANK HIM . . .

I'M SORRY ABOUT DEFENDER, BUDDY. DO ***YOU*** WANT TO GO UP THERE AND SAY SOMETHING?

I DON'T KNOW ***WHAT*** TO SAY.

I'M ***CAPTAIN RAMSEY.*** IT'S NO SECRET THAT DEFENDER AND I HAD OUR ***DIFFERENCES.*** BUT HE SAVED MY LIFE MORE TIMES THAN I CAN COUNT. AND . . . I . . .
I'M SORRY. I HAVE NO WORDS.
REMEMBER

SEE YOU NEXT WEEKEND, ANDREW?
HE'LL BE FINE. HE JUST NEEDS TIME.

LATER.
WANT ME TO MAKE YOU A PEANUT-BUTTER-AND-BANANA SANDWICH? IT'S YOUR FAVORITE!
NO, THANKS.

MY GAME'S ON PAUSE, SO DON'T TOUCH IT!
SURE THING.

AND DON'T USE THE PHONE! I'M WAITING FOR A CALL!
NO PROBLEM.

IS ANDREW OK? HE DIDN'T EVEN PUT UP A FIGHT!
HE'S VERY SAD RIGHT NOW, TOMMY.

HEY, ANDREW—I PICKED UP THE NEW DEFENDER COMIC, IF YOU WANT TO READ IT.
COOL, THANKS.

TAKE AS LONG AS YOU WANT. I DON'T NEED IT BACK RIGHT AWAY.

WISH I COULD TELL SOMEONE ABOUT MY POWERS.

DEFENDER

BUT I CAN'T TRUST TOMMY, AND IF I TOLD MOM AND DAD, THEY'D BE SO WORRIED THAT THEY WOULDN'T LET ME LEAVE MY ROOM FOR THE REST OF MY LIFE!

WHY DID I GET THESE POWERS?
WHAP!
WHY NOT A COP LIKE CAPTAIN RAMSEY? OR A FIREMAN? OR SOMEONE WHO'S OLD ENOUGH TO SHAVE?

I MEAN, WHAT GOOD IS A LITTLE KID WHO CAN FLY AND RUN FAST?
BOING!

OH, YEAH— AND HAS SUPER STRENGTH?

I DON'T EVEN KNOW HOW STRONG I AM!
THUNK!

I'M STILL IN ELEMENTARY SCHOOL. . . . I CAN'T DRIVE . . . I CAN'T STAY OUT PAST EIGHT ON A SCHOOL NIGHT!
I COULD NEVER BE THE KIND OF HERO YOU WERE!

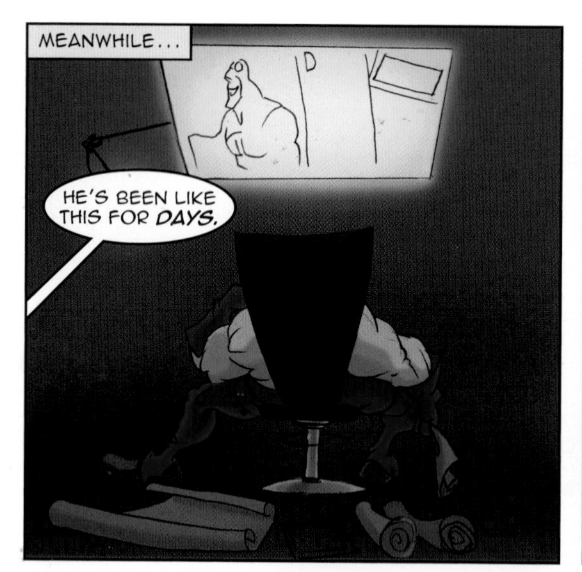
MEANWHILE . . .
HE'S BEEN LIKE THIS FOR *DAYS.*

HE DOESN'T SLEEP. WON'T EAT. I'D TRY TALKING TO HIM, BUT I'M AFRAID FOR MY *LIFE.*
BEST LET *ME* HANDLE THIS.
I DON'T KNOW, DOC. HE SAID HE DOESN'T WANT TO BE BOTHERED . . .

NOT TO WORRY. I HAVE JUST THE THING TO CHEER HIM UP!
SERIOUSLY, I DON'T THINK NOW'S A GOOD—

MAGUS, OLD CHUM! YOUR LONGTIME ENEMY IS FINALLY BEATEN! LET'S CELEBRATE!

TELL ME SOMETHING, DR. WILSON . . .
POP!

I HIRED YOU TO BUILD A DEVICE THAT WOULD **ABSORB** DEFENDER'S POWERS AND TRANSFER THEM TO **ME.** INSTEAD, YOUR MACHINE MALFUNCTIONED AND **KILLED** HIM.
DEFENDER'S POWERS ARE **LOST** FOREVER. SO, JUST OUT OF CURIOSITY . . .

WHAT ARE WE **CELEBRATING?** MY **MISERY?** OR YOUR **INCOMPETENCE?**

I WARNED YOU IT WAS JUST A PROTOTYPE AND TOO SOON TO—
URK

WILSON . . . YOU'RE **FIRED.**

NO! WAIT! **PLEEEEEEASE!**

YEAH, GOTTA BABYSIT MY KID BROTHER WHILE MOM'S AT WORK . . .
. . . HOSTAGE SITUATION AT SEATOWN NATIONAL BANK!

FOUR ARMED GUNMEN BURST IN A HALF HOUR AGO AND TOOK SEVERAL HOSTAGES.
BANK

HEY, ANDREW, DAD WANTS YOU TO CALL HIM WHEN I'M OFF THE PHONE.
POLICE HAVE THE BANK COMPLETELY SURROUNDED. SO FAR, THE GUNMEN HAVE ISSUED NO LIST OF DEMANDS.

YO, ANDREW? ANYBODY HOME?
HOSTAGES? IF ONLY DEFENDER WAS ALIVE, HE'D USE HIS POWERS TO . . .

WAIT. THEY'RE MY POWERS NOW!

I STILL HAVE THAT **COSTUME** MOM MADE ME FOR **HALLOWEEN!**

WHERE IS IT? IT'S GOTTA BE . . . **AHA!**

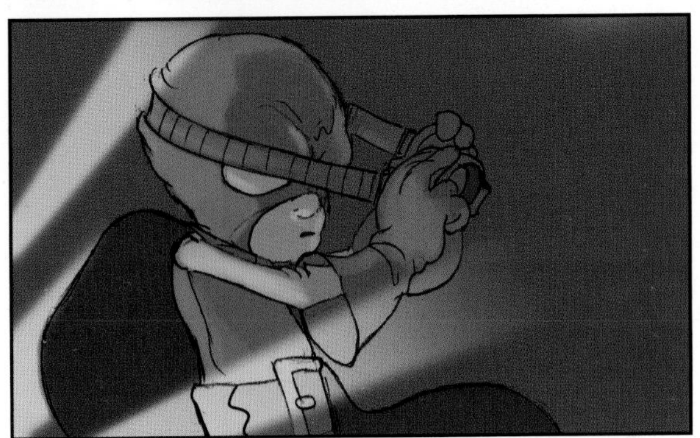

WHAP!
OUCH!

HEY, BRO! WANNA MAKE COOKIES? I BOUGHT SOME FROZEN CHOCOLATE-CHIP COOKIE DOUGH . . .

ANDREW?

THIS MIGHT BE THE CRAZIEST, DUMBEST THING I'VE EVER DONE!

BUT IF I REALLY *DO* HAVE DEFENDER'S POWERS . . . I GUESS IT'S UP TO *ME* TO USE THEM FOR GOOD!

MAYBE I'M NOT THE *BEST* GUY FOR THE JOB . . . BUT I'M THE *ONLY* GUY!
WHOOSH!!

WOOOOOO-HOOOOOOOOOOO!!!!!
NOW I JUST NEED MY OWN THEME MUSIC!
AND I CAN BE SPARROWHAWK— FOR REAL!

HOLY MONKEY! DIDN'T REALIZE I WAS UP SO HIGH!
DON'T LOOK DOWN! AND DON'T PANIC! JUST GRAB SOMETHING . . .

ALMOST GOT IT . . . JUST A LITTLE CLOSER . . .

WELL, THAT WASN'T SO HARD! NOW I JUST NEED TO GET DOWN . . .

HOW HUMILIATING! I BET DEFENDER WASN'T AFRAID OF HEIGHTS!

EASY, NOW . . . DOING GOOD, DOING FINE . . .
GAAHH!
WHOOPS, SORRY TO BOTHER YOU!
CRUNCH!
HERE WE GO, NICE AND SOFT . . .
NOW I'LL STAY LOW . . .

EXCUSE ME, FOLKS!
DOES ANYONE KNOW
WHERE SEATOWN
NATIONAL BANK IS?

STEP ASIDE! OUTTA
THE WAY! SUPERHERO
COMING THROUGH!

NEVER MIND,
I'LL GO AROUND!

UH-OH!
WRONG WAY!

BA-DOOM!

WAY TO MAKE A GREAT
FIRST IMPRESSION!

I NEED TO GET A MAP, OR GPS— OR SOMETHING!
STOP

YO! CAN'T YOU READ THE SIGN? THINK I'M STANDIN' HERE FOR FUN?
OOPS, SORRY!

SAY, YOU DON'T KNOW WHERE I CAN FIND MIDTOWN—

SMASH!
OOF!

BETTER TAKE SOME FLYIN' LESSONS . . . SMASH! HAW HAW HAW HAW!
GEEZ, THAT DIDN'T EVEN HURT! WELL, EXCEPT FOR MY PRIDE . . .

WEEOOWEEOOWEEOOWEEOO!
NOW HOW AM I SUPPOSED TO FIND THE—?
AHA! FOLLOW THAT CAR!

SLOW DOWN, PETE! YOU'RE GIVIN' ME WHIPLASH!
DEFENDER TOOK A DIRT NAP, SO IT'S UP TO US COPS TO WIPE THESE SCUMBAGS OFF THE STREET, PAULIE!

I AIN'T MISSIN' A SECOND OF THIS—HUH?

WHAT THE—?

LOOK OUT, YOU MANIAC!

AW, GEEZ!
SCREEEEEEEEEEEEEEEEEEECH!

WHY DID THEY STOP? DID THEY *SEE* ME?

WHEW!
I WANT A NEW PARTNER . . .

THAT WAS *CLOSE!* GOOD THING NOBODY GOT—

HURT!

NO BRAKES!
CRASH!!

I'VE REALLY GOTTA WORK ON MY LANDINGS!
WHUMP!
AND MY TAKEOFFS!

AND FLYING IN GENERAL . . .

MAYBE NEXT TIME I CAN MAKE SOME MORE NOISE! WAY TO SNEAK IN, ANDREW!
THUD!
JUST HOPE I DIDN'T ALERT THE . . .

. . . BANK ROBBERS?
IT'S JUST A . . . KID?
HELLO, LITTLE MAN! HOW'D YOU GET IN HERE?

I WAS, UM, H-HIDING FROM MY **MOM** ON THE ROOF! I **SLIPPED** A—AND FELL THROUGH THE WINDOW!

I SAY **SHOOT** HIM, TO BE **SAFE!**
HE'S JUST A KID, YOU NINNY!
PUT HIM WITH THE **OTHERS** FOR NOW.

WELL, **THIS** DIDN'T WORK OUT LIKE I'D PLANNED!
WONDER IF **DEFENDER** STARTED OUT LIKE THIS!

I DON'T **LIKE** THIS. HE COULD BE A **COP!**
THE POLICE ACADEMY'S GOT A **KINDERGARTEN** NOW?
RELAX, THE EXPLOSIVES ARE SET.

YOU PUSH THE BUTTON AND IT ALL GOES **BOOM!**

THIS WAY, KID!
SWEET, **SASSY** CRAP!

THESE GUYS HAVE MORE EXPLOSIVES THAN **WILE E. COYOTE!**

NOT **ANOTHER** ONE!
IT'S A LITTLE **KID!**
WHERE DID **HE** COME FROM?!

HERE YA GO, BRAT. GET COMFY.

IT'S OK. YOU'RE SAFE HERE WITH US!
I'VE GOTTA GET THESE PEOPLE OUT OF HERE . . .

SAFE? THOSE GOONS WILL LET US GO OVER THEIR DEAD BODIES!

DON'T SAY THAT. YOU'LL SCARE HIM!
HEY, UH . . . WHERE DOES THAT **VENT** GO?

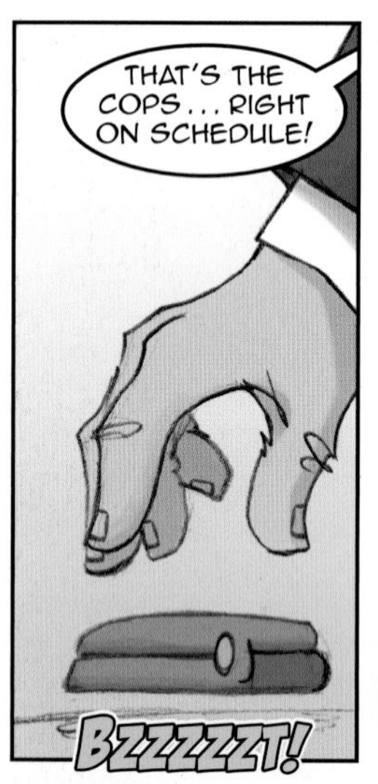
THAT'S THE COPS . . . RIGHT ON SCHEDULE!
BZZZZZZT!

BANK ROBBER SPEAKING. WHO'S CALLING, PLEASE?

THIS IS CAPTAIN RAMSEY OF THE SEATOWN POLICE DEPARTMENT. LET THE HOSTAGES GO, AND WE'LL DISCUSS YOUR DEMANDS.

I WANT ALL COPS CLEARED OUT IN ONE HOUR, INCLUDING THOSE SNIPERS ON THE ROOFTOPS!

BUT THE HOSTAGES— HELLO? HELLO?

HE HUNG UP.
SIR! SNIPERS SAW THE PERSON WHO FLEW THROUGH THAT WINDOW! THEY SAID IT LOOKED . . .

B NK
LIKE DEFENDER!
WE CAN ONLY PRAY IT'S HIM.

BATHROOM BREAK, FOLKS! LINE UP, ONE AT A—

WHERE'D THEY GO?

WHUP WHUP WHUP
COME ON, HURRY UP!
WHERE'S THAT KID?

HERE GOES NOTHIN'!
CODE RED!

GANGWAY!
WHUMP!

WHEW! THAT WASN'T SO HARD.
THUD!

MICK! WHAT'S GOIN' ON, MAN—
THIS'LL BE TROUBLE . . .

BUDABUDABUDABUDABUDABUDABUDA

IT'S THAT BRAT! I KNEW HE WAS TROUBLE!
MAN, THAT'S CRAZY TALK! WHAT COULD A LITTLE KID DO?

THIS BETTER WORK!
CRASH!

THE TABLE— IT'S ATTACKING US?!
SHUT UP AN' SHOOT!
BUDABUDABUDA
BLAM!
BLAM!
BLAM!

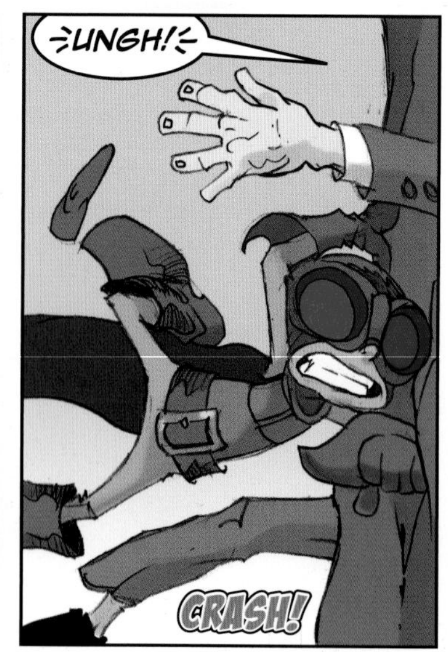
UNGH!
CRASH!

IT WORKED! I'M ALIVE! I THINK...
I'D BETTER GET OUTTA HERE BEFORE—

NOT ANOTHER STEP OR IT'S BYE-BYE, PUBERTY!
IT WAS AN ACCIDENT, I SWEAR!
STEP AWAY SLOWLY. . . .

NO, WAIT. STOP! DON'T TAKE ANOTHER—
CRUNCH!
—STEP!

DEET!
DEET!

BEEEEEEEEEP!

BA-DA-DOOM!!

THINGS KEEP BLOWIN' UP AROUND HERE!

SOMEBODY'S MOVING....
YOU IN THE BANK!

KEEP YOUR HANDS IN THE AIR! COME OUT NOW, OR WE'LL SHOOT!

SOMEONE'S COMING!

KOFF! KOFF!

WHAT THE—?
IS—IS THAT... A KID?

I GOT THE MAIN GUY HERE! THE OTHERS ARE INSIDE. EVERYBODY'S STILL ALIVE, BUT THE BANK'S GONNA NEED SOME NEW PAINT AND STUFF.

NO NEED TO THANK ME. JUST DOING MY JOB!

BE SEEIN' YA! THE NAME'S ***SPARROWHAWK,*** BY THE WAY.

WAIT! COME BACK!
WHAT WAS YOUR **NAME** AGAIN?
HOW **OLD** ARE YOU?
ARE YOU **RELATED** TO DEFENDER?

CAPTAIN! THE HOSTAGES ARE ALL SAFE! CAPTAIN?
THAT CAN'T BE DEFENDER! HE'S ***DEAD!*** UNLESS THE MAGUS SHRANK HIM SOMEHOW.

LATER THAT NIGHT.
CHANNEL FOUR SPOKE TO WITNESSES WHO SAW THE COSTUMED HERO IN *ACTION!*
THIS KID IN HIS JAMMIES FLIES RIGHT PAST ME AND—*SMASH!* HITS A STEEL *GIRDER.*
I'M ALL LIKE, "WAY TO GO, *SMASH!*" HAW-HAW!

THAT OUGHTA BE HIS NAME . . . *SMASH!* HAW-HAW!
THAT'S *ME* THEY'RE TALKING ABOUT! I'M *FAMOUS!*
I'M *COOL* . . .

STUPID *JERK!* IF YOU SNEAK OUT AND GET HURT, *I* GET BUSTED!
SORRY, TOMMY! I DIDN'T MEAN TO—
IF MOM FINDS OUT AND I GET GROUNDED, *I SWEAR* . . .

WHAT ARE YOU TWO DOING UP? IT'S *MIDNIGHT!*
GET TO BED RIGHT NOW, *BOTH* OF YOU— OR NO TV FOR A *WEEK!*

MAGUS'S HEADQUARTERS.
SIR! I APOLOGIZE FOR INTRUDING—

. . . BUT YOU HAVE TO SEE WHAT'S ON THE NEWS.

. . . HOSTAGE SITUATION WAS APPARENTLY FOILED BY THIS UNNAMED FIGURE.

THE HOSTAGES TELL A REMARKABLE STORY OF COURAGE . . .
THIS LITTLE BOY IN HIS PAJAMAS FLEW US UP TO A VENT! THANKS TO HIM, WE ALL GOT OUT BEFORE THE BOMB WENT OFF!
POLICE OFFICIALS ARE BAFFLED BY THE INCIDENT AND CLAIM THEY KNOW NOTHING ABOUT THE YOUNG HERO . . .
I WANT TO SEE DR. COBB.

THE NEXT MORNING.
WHAT THE . . . ?
"SMASH" BUSTS HOLDUP!
Costumed Kid frees hostages.
CAPTURES ROBBERS!

I COME UP WITH A COOL NAME LIKE SPARROWHAWK— AND THE PRESS CALLS ME "SMASH"!

LATER.
NONE OF THESE KIDS HAS ANY IDEA THERE'S A HERO SITTING AMONG THEM!

AT RECESS.
CAN'T CATCH ME, MAGUS!
I WANNA BE SMASH THIS TIME!
EVERYONE WANTS TO BE ME!

HEADS UP!
WHANG!

NOWHERE TO RUN THIS TIME, WIMP!
LET'S FINISH WHAT WE STARTED!
TIME TO GET POUNDED!

WITH MY POWERS, I COULD WHIP ALL THREE OF THEM RIGHT HERE AND NOW!
READY WHEN YOU ARE, GARETH!

BUT THEN, EVERYBODY WOULD KNOW ABOUT MY POWERS! MY SECRET IDENTITY WOULDN'T BE SECRET ANYMORE.
IS HE REALLY GONNA DO IT?
NAH, HE'LL RUN AWAY . . .

ON THE OTHER HAND, GARETH, I'M WILLING TO FORGET ABOUT THE GUM IN MY HAIR, MY WRECKED BIKE—ALL THAT STUFF—WHAT DO YOU SAY?

I SAY . . .
WHAP!
HUUUH!

WOW! I BARELY EVEN FELT THAT! BUT I'D BETTER PLAY ALONG . . .
NO! S-STAY AWAY! L-LEAVE ME ALONE!

THIS IS WHAT HAPPENS WHEN YOU TRY TO RUN FROM ME!
YEAH! THIS IS WHAT HAPPENS!

WHAT'S GOING **ON** HERE? SAVE IT FOR P.E. CLASS, **BREEDLOVE!**
YOU BOYS SEEM INCAPABLE OF KEEPING YOUR HANDS TO YOURSELVES.

I DIDN'T DO ANYTHING! **ANDREW** STARTED IT!
SOMEHOW, I **DOUBT** THAT. LET'S SEE IF YOUR PARENTS BELIEVE YOU!

ANDREW, ARE YOU ALL RIGHT?
DON'T CALL MY MOM! I BEG YOU!
SAVE IT, TOUGH GUY!
YEAH, I FEEL **GREAT!** UH, I MEAN, IT DOESN'T HURT **TOO** MUCH . . .

YOU **REALLY** STOOD UP TO GARETH!
WAY TO **GO,** ANDREW!
I WAS ROOTING FOR **YOU** THE WHOLE TIME!

WHO KNEW I COULD **WIN** WITHOUT EVEN **FIGHTING?**

LATER.
FEELS **STRANGE** . . . LIKE I DON'T HAVE TO BE SCARED OF **ANYTHING,** EVER AGAIN!

AND NOW, A LOOK AT SMASH! SOME SAY HE'S ONLY A CHILD AND SHOULD BE STOPPED BEFORE HE HURTS HIMSELF . . .
AW, C'MON!— SMASH?

WHILE OTHER EXPERTS MAINTAIN HE'S JUST A VERY SHORT PERSON . . .

HEY! WHERE ARE YOU GOING THIS LATE, TOMMY?

MOM SAID YOU'RE GROUNDED! PLUS, YOU'RE NOT SUPPOSED TO GO OUT ON SCHOOL NIGHTS.

SHUT UP, YOU LITTLE JERK! YOU AREN'T THE BOSS OF ME—NOBODY IS!
AND IT'S TOM. NOT TOMMY! GOT IT?

SLAM!

OOOOOOKAAAAY . . . THAT WAS INTENSE!

MOMENTS LATER.
MOM WILL GET OFF WORK IN AN HOUR, SO I CAN'T STAY OUT TOO LATE . . .

BUT I HAVE TO FIND OUT WHERE TOMMY'S GOING! I MEAN . . . TOM.
I HAVE TO MAKE SURE HE STAYS OUT OF TROUBLE.

HEY, IF HE DOES GET INTO TROUBLE, I COULD RESCUE HIM. THAT'D BE PRETTY COOL!
WHO ARE THOSE GUYS? OH, YEAH . . . HIS JERK FRIENDS!

WHY DOES HE HANG OUT WITH PUNKS LIKE THAT? I SHOULD FLY DOWN AND GIVE THEM A SCARE—

BOOM!
WHAT THE—?

BETTER MAKE THIS QUICK SO I DON'T LOSE TRACK OF TOM!

ANOTHER BANK ROBBERY! THESE GUYS **NEVER** LEARN . . .

YOU GUYS GET ONE CHANCE TO SURRENDER, OR ELSE WE DO THIS THE HARD WAY!

UH . . . YOU KNOW, BY "HARD WAY," I MEANT HARD FOR **YOU!** YOU **GOT** THAT, RIGHT?

WHOA! ONE **HARD WAY** COMIN' RIGHT UP!
POPPAPOPPAPOPPAPOPPAPOPPA!

CLANG!
OW, MY **HAND!**

DID THAT GUY'S **FACE** JUST GO **"CLANG"?**

ROBOTS! WHAT DO YOU NEED MONEY FOR?!

WAIT A MINUTE . . . ROBOTS?!

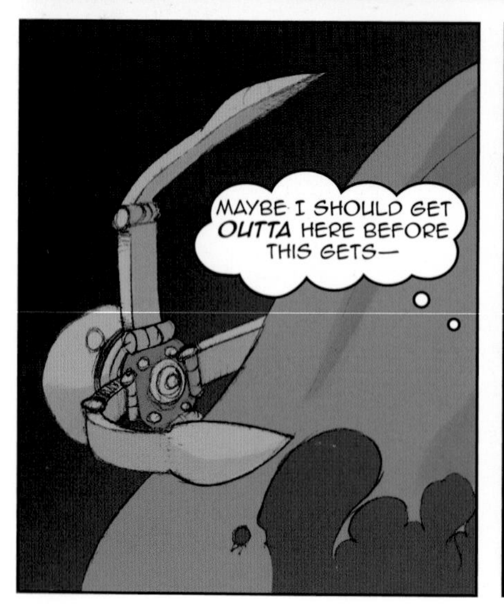
MAYBE I SHOULD GET OUTTA HERE BEFORE THIS GETS—

GAKK!

TOO LATE!

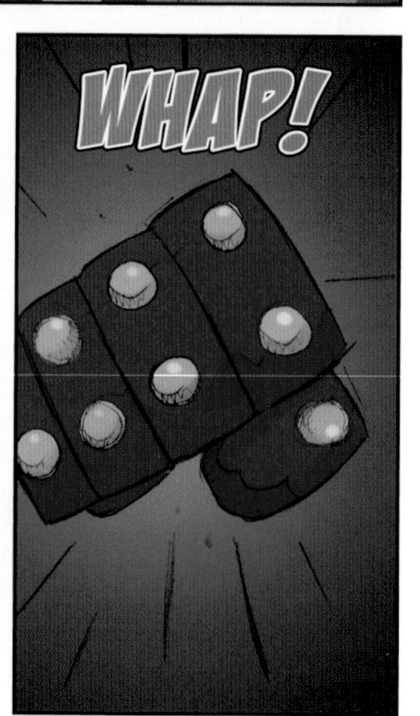
WHAP!

THUD!

OK, *THAT* HURT.

MAYBE IT'S A LITTLE SOON FOR ME TO TACKLE A TRIO OF *ROBOTS!* I'LL COME BACK WHEN I'VE HAD SOME MORE—

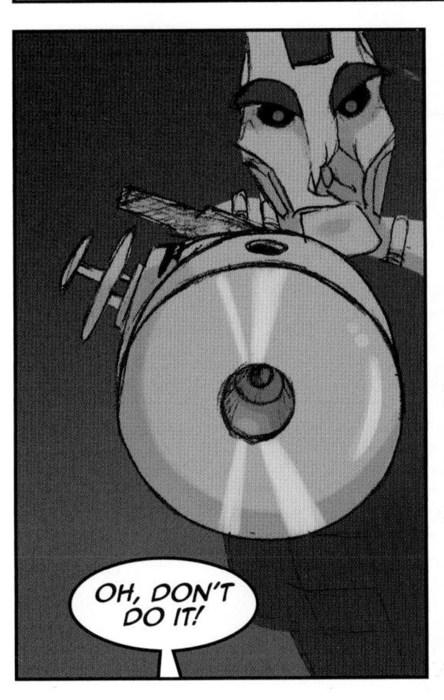
OH, DON'T DO IT!

POPPAPOPPAPOPPAPOPPAPOPPAPOPPA
YAAAAAAHHHH!

WELL, THIS STINKS!

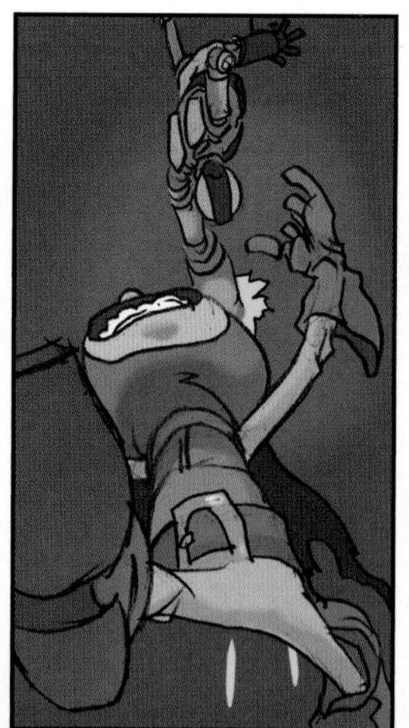

FIRST, TAKE OUT THE MACHINE GUN! THEN, IF I'M NOT DEAD, WORRY ABOUT THE OTHER TWO!

KUNG!

CRIPES, I'M STUCK! GIVE ME BACK MY HAND, YOU METAL FREAK!

UH-OH!

RRRRAAAAGH!
POPPAPOPPAPOPPAPOPPAPOPPA

PING!
PING!
PING!
PING!
PING!
PING!
POPPAPOPPAPOPPAPOPPAPOPPAPOPPAPOPPAPOPPAPOPPAPOP

HOW DO I SHUT THIS GUN OFF?
POPPAPOPPAPOPPA

SHUNK!
THERE!

BACK TO THE SCRAP HEAP!

WELL, I GUESS *THAT'S* OVER WITH.
I'D BETTER GET HOME BEFORE MOM FLIPS OUT!
KER-ESH!
CRUNCH!

IF I CAN JUST GET THIS STUPID HEAD OFF MY HAND!

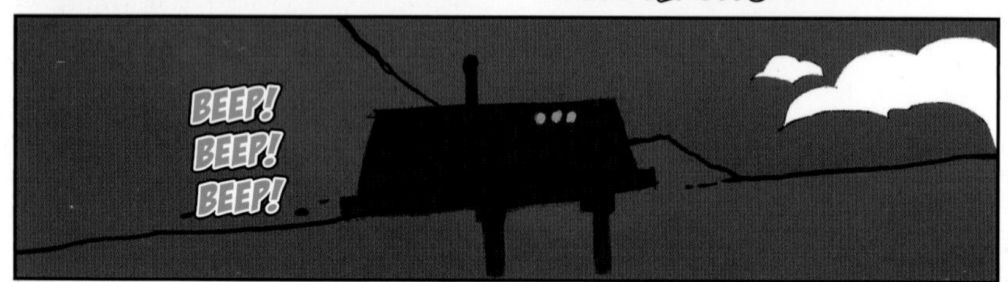
BEEP! BEEP! BEEP!

ELSEWHERE.
MOST *IMPRESSIVE.*

CRUDE, YES. *CLUMSY,* EVEN.
YET QUITE *EFFECTIVE.* THE BOY *INTRIGUES* ME.
THIS ENCOUNTER HAS GIVEN US PLENTY OF DATA, SIR.

BY TOMORROW MORNING, I SHOULD HAVE A *FULL REPORT.*

NOW, SMASH . . . WE'RE GOING TO FIND OUT *WHAT* YOU'RE REALLY MADE OF.

THE RYANS' HOUSE.
MOM, CAN YOU PATCH UP MY DEFENDER COSTUME?
I, UH, **FELL DOWN** AND IT GOT A LITTLE RIPPED.

IT'S **RUINED!** WE SHOULD THROW IT OUT. I CAN MAKE YOU A **NEW COSTUME** NEXT YEAR—
JUST SEW THIS ONE UP. IT'LL BE **FINE!**

ANDREW! YOU—YOU'RE **SMASH?**

HEH, HEH! C'MON, TOM, YOU'RE TALKING LIKE A **LOONY!**
ALSO, HIS NAME **ISN'T** SMASH, IT'S SPARROWHAWK! AND I'M DEFINITELY **NOT** HIM!

YOUNG MAN, YOU ARE **GROUNDED!** NO FIGHTING CRIME FOR A **WEEK!** AND NO TV, EITHER!

BOOM!!
OH, NO...

THE MAGUS!

WELL, WELL, WELL! WHAT HAVE WE HERE?
I SMELL THE BLOOD OF A SUPERHERO...

ANDREW, HELP! USE YOUR POWERS!
ANDREW, SAVE US!

DON'T HURT MY FAMILY, MAGUS!

YOU'RE GOING TO BE EVEN EASIER TO KILL THAN DEFENDER!

NOOOOOOOOOOOOOOOOOOO!
ANDREW! ARE YOU ALL RIGHT?

THAT MUST HAVE BEEN SOME NIGHTMARE!
IT SEEMED SO REAL . . .

WELL, YOU'RE OK NOW. DO YOU REMEMBER WHAT IT WAS ABOUT?
UH . . . I FORGET. I'M JUST GLAD YOU'RE— I MEAN, I'M SAFE!

TRY TO GO BACK TO SLEEP, HONEY. WHERE'S THAT COSTUME YOU WANTED ME TO MEND?

COSTUME? WHAT COSTUME? HEY, WOULDJA LOOK AT THE TIME, I BETTER GET SOME Z'S! NUH-NIGHT, MOM!
UH, OK. SWEET DREAMS . . . ?

WHEW! CLOSE ONE! I'D BETTER FIGURE OUT HOW TO SEW . . .

LAB OF DR. COBB.
OH, BABY!

FOOM!!
FEEL THAT POWER! NOW THAT'S WHAT I'M TALKIN' ABOUT!
ABOUT MY FEE, MISTER—
JUST CALL ME PULSE!

THESE BLASTERS ARE GREAT, COBB! WORTH EVERY PENNY!
FOR ANOTHER FIFTY THOUSAND, I OFFER A FULL FIVE-YEAR WARRANTY . . .

WHOA! WHAT'S WITH HIM?

EASY, BRUTE.
IT SEEMS WE HAVE . . . UNEXPECTED COMPANY.

GOOD EVENING, DR. COBB.
I HAVE BUSINESS TO DISCUSS WITH YOU. ALONE.

THANKS FOR THE SUIT, COBB. I WAS JUST ON MY WAY OUT!

AS I RECALL, MAGUS, OUR LAST MEETING DIDN'T END ON THE BEST OF TERMS.
I DON'T BELIEVE IN HOLDING GRUDGES, DOCTOR.

NEITHER DO I, BUT I'M AFRAID BRUTE DOES. PERHAPS YOU SHOULD GET TO THE POINT.
I WANT YOU TO BUILD A MACHINE FOR ME.
A DEVICE THAT WILL REMOVE A PERSON'S POWERS AND STORE THEM FOR SAFEKEEPING.

I WILL, OF COURSE, PAY **HANDSOMELY** FOR IT!

IF AT FIRST YOU DON'T **SUCCEED,** EH? AN **INTRIGUING** PROPOSITION . . .

VERY WELL. I **ACCEPT** YOUR OFFER.

ONE MORE THING, COBB. I'M **NOT** BUYING A **WARRANTY.** MAKE SURE IT WORKS RIGHT THE **FIRST** TIME!
DISAPPOINT ME . . .

AND EVEN YOUR **GORILLA** WON'T BE ABLE TO SAVE YOU!

POLICE HEADQUARTERS.

EXCUSE ME, CAPTAIN RAMSEY...
IT'S LATE, DETECTIVE DORIX. WHAT DO YOU NEED?

ACTUALLY, SIR, IT'S PRONOUNCED DOOR-OH.
OR DOOR-OOH, IF YOU PREFER THE FRENCH—

DID YOU COME IN HERE TO TELL ME HOW TO SAY YOUR NAME?
NO, SIR. I'M WRITING MY REPORT ON THE DEFENDER CASE...

SERGEANT HALSEY HEARD YOU TELL DEFENDER THAT YOU HAVE A "MAN ON THE INSIDE." IF THERE'S A COP WORKING UNDERCOVER AS A MINION...

I'D LIKE TO TALK TO HIM ABOUT HIS TIP ON THE MAGUS.

"UNDERCOVER" MEANS HIS IDENTITY STAYS A SECRET.
WELL, SINCE THIS IS MY CASE, I'LL NEED TO—

THE CASE IS CLOSED, DETECTIVE!
DEFENDER IS DEAD. THE MAGUS KILLED HIM. END OF STORY! GOT IT?

YEAH, CAPTAIN. I GOT IT.

STUPID, NOSY DETECTIVES!
ALWAYS SNIFFING AROUND . . .
JUST LIKE I USED TO!

DOUROUX'S LIKE A SHARK THAT SMELLS BLOOD. HE WON'T LET UP, NO MATTER HOW MUCH I—

EXCUSE ME, CAPTAIN . . .
MIGHT I HAVE A WORD WITH YOU?

ARE YOU CRAZY, COMING HERE?! SOMEONE MIGHT SEE US!

THEN I SUGGEST YOU GET IN.

I THOUGHT OUR DEAL WAS FINISHED! YOU GOT WHAT YOU WANTED.

I'M AFRAID NOT. IT SEEMS DEFENDER'S POWERS HAVE FOUND A NEW HOME—NOT IN ME, BUT IN THE BODY OF A CHILD!
THIS IS UNACCEPTABLE.

NOT MY PROBLEM, MAGUS! YOU BOTCHED YOUR LITTLE SCIENCE PROJECT, NOT ME! YOU WANTED ME TO DELIVER DEFENDER TO YOU, AND I DID.

I DIDN'T COME HERE TO ARGUE WITH YOU, RAMSEY. I CAME TO CONVINCE YOU.

WHAT IS THIS?
DEFENDER HAS BEEN A THORN IN BOTH OUR SIDES FOR TOO LONG. IF YOU HELP ME, I GUARANTEE YOU CAN GO ON LIVING A HAPPY, PEACEFUL LIFE AS A POLICE CAPTAIN.

ARE YOU THREATENING ME, MAGUS?
WHY, NOTHING OF THE SORT! I'M MERELY CONCERNED FOR THE SAFETY OF YOUR ADORABLE FAMILY.

I ASSURE YOU, MY ONLY INTEREST IS IN TAKING DEFENDER'S POWERS.
AND ONCE THIS MATTER IS CLOSED, YOU WON'T HEAR FROM ME AGAIN.
WHATEVER IT TAKES, MAGUS!

I'M CURIOUS HOW MANY HITS THIS VIDEO WOULD GET ONLINE. I THINK IT MIGHT GO VIRAL.
WE HAVE COPIES READY TO SEND TO LOCAL NEWS STATIONS. THE DIGITAL REPRODUCTION IS SUPERB!

WHAT DO YOU THINK?

I'LL BE IN TOUCH . . .
DEAR GOD . . . WHAT HAVE I DONE?

MEANWHILE . . .
GOTTA GET OVER MY FEAR OF HEIGHTS IF I'M GOING TO BE ANY KIND OF SUPERHERO.
I FLEW UP FOUR FLOORS, SO TWENTY MORE SHOULDN'T BE A BIG DEAL . . . RIGHT?

EVEN THOUGH IT'S SUCH A LOOOOONG WAY TO FALL . . .

ALL RIGHT! NO GUTS, NO GLORY! IT'S FLYIN' TIME!
ON THREE! ONE, TWO . . . OK, WAIT. EENIE, MEENIE, MINEY . . . NO, THAT'S NO GOOD. OK . . . HERE IT COMES . . .
AAAAAAND . . . AWAY . . . WE . . .

GO!

DON'T LOOK DOWN! DON'T EVEN THINK ABOUT WHAT'S NOT UNDER YOU!

I CAN'T BELIEVE IT . . . I'M ALMOST TO THE ROOF!

I'M GONNA MAKE IT! WHAT WAS I SO SCARED OF, ANYWAY?

WHUNFFF!

BIIIIIIRDS!
HELP! I'M FALLING! SOMEBODY CATCH ME!

DON'T FREAK OUT! YOU CAN FIX THIS! JUST START FLYING . . . C'MON, FLY! WHY WON'T YOU FLY ALREADY?

IF I CAN GRAB AHOLD OF THIS BILLBOARD . . .
UH
OS

CRASH!!

GUESS I NEED SOME MORE PRACTICE. . . .

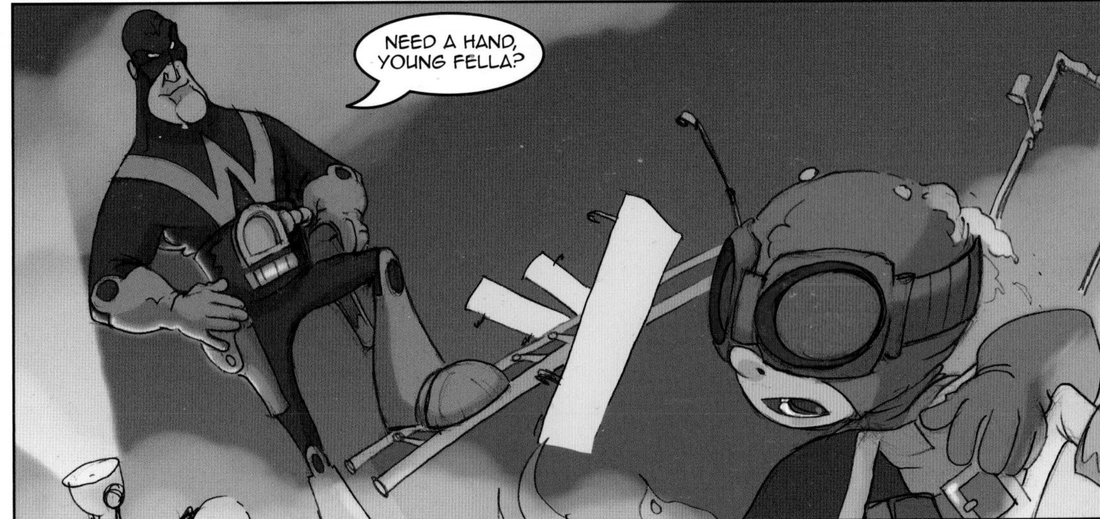
NEED A HAND, YOUNG FELLA?

WELL, LOOKIE HERE—MY FIRST SUPER-VILLAIN! AND JUST WHO ARE YOU SUPPOSED TO BE?

YOU'RE JOKING, RIGHT? I'M THE WRAITH! YOU MUST HAVE HEARD OF ME!
YOU MEAN "WRATH"? LIKE "WRATH OF KHAN"?
UH, NO . . . ACTUALLY, I DON'T . . .

"KHAAAAAAAAN!"
NO, NO . . .
"DO YOU HEAR ME, KHAN? DO YOU?"
NO KHAN, NOT KHAN!

WRAITH, PERIOD! LIKE A GHOST. LIKE I CAN PASS THROUGH SOLID OBJECTS!

YOU'VE NEVER HEARD OF ME?
ARE YOU NEW IN TOWN?
ARE YOU KIDDING ME? I'M A HERO! I'M A LEGEND!

"I STARTED IN THE '60S. USING ATOMIC-AGE SCIENCE, I DESIGNED A SUIT THAT WOULD ENABLE ME TO PHASE THROUGH ANY SURFACE AND MATERIALIZE ON THE OTHER SIDE!"
"AS MY CAREER CONTINUED INTO THE '70S, I DEVELOPED A NOTORIOUS ROGUES' GALLERY, INCLUDING MAN-CAT, MIRRORBALL, AND THE ROLLER TWINS!"

"BY THE LATE '80S, ALL OF THEM WERE RETIRED OR IN PRISON. THE LUCKY ONES, ANYWAY. AS TIMES CHANGED, THERE SEEMED LESS OF A NEED FOR SOMEONE LIKE ME TO FIGHT CRIME."

WAAAAIT, I READ ABOUT YOU! YOU FOUGHT DEFENDER BACK IN THE '90S! MAN, HE KICKED YOUR BUTT . . .
IT WAS A SIMPLE MISUNDERSTANDING CAUSED BY THE MAGUS!

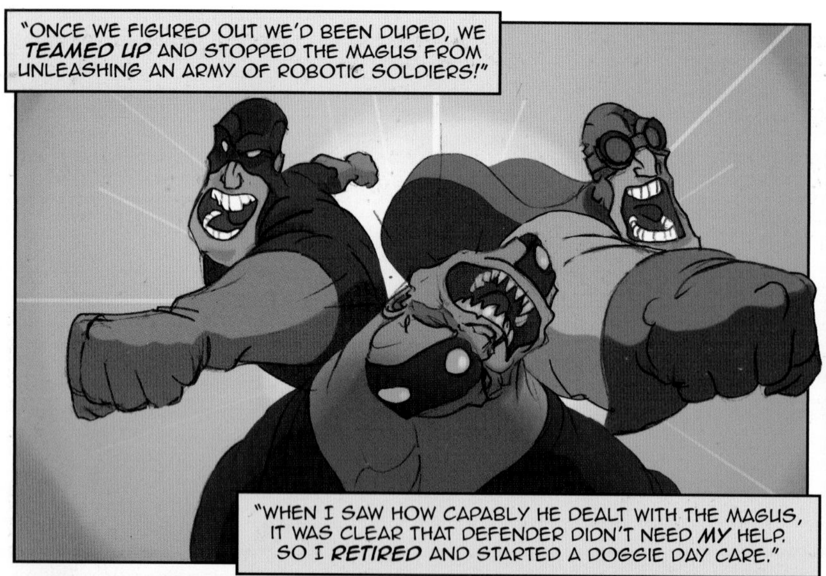
"ONCE WE FIGURED OUT WE'D BEEN DUPED, WE TEAMED UP AND STOPPED THE MAGUS FROM UNLEASHING AN ARMY OF ROBOTIC SOLDIERS!"
"WHEN I SAW HOW CAPABLY HE DEALT WITH THE MAGUS, IT WAS CLEAR THAT DEFENDER DIDN'T NEED MY HELP. SO I RETIRED AND STARTED A DOGGIE DAY CARE."

BUT NOW, HE'S GONE... AND I'M NEEDED AGAIN.
NO WORRIES, OLD-TIMER...

I'M HERE TO PICK UP WHERE DEFENDER LEFT OFF!
YOU'RE TOO YOUNG.

WHADDAYA MEAN, "TOO YOUNG"? HAVE YOU SEEN WHAT I CAN DO?

YEAH, I'VE SEEN YOU FLY AROUND AND SMASH INTO THINGS. YOU NEED TRAINING AND EXPERIENCE. WE'LL START YOU AS MY SIDEKICK SO YOU CAN STUDY MY MOVES —
NO WAY! SIDEKICKS SPEW! BESIDES, YOU'RE TOO OLD TO TEACH ME ANYTHING!
OH, YOU THINK SO? WELL...

AM I TOO OLD FOR THIS?
WHAP!

TOO OLD TO PUNCH A WALL?
OHHHH . . . THAT WAS SUPPOSED TO GO THROUGH THE WALL!

MY SUIT JUST NEEDS A TUNE-UP— THE PHASING IS ON THE FRITZ!
CAREFUL. DON'T BREAK YOUR HIP!
MY KNUCKLES SCREAM . . .

THANKS FOR THE OFFER, GRAMPS, BUT I'M GETTING THE HANG OF THINGS JUST FINE!
WAIT! YOU REALLY DO NEED HELP. YOU'RE A DANGER TO YOURSELF—AND OTHERS!

WHAT DOES THAT OLD GUY KNOW? I'LL SHOW HIM WHO'S TOO YOUNG!
CAN YOU BRING ME AN ICE PACK . . . ?

THE MAGUS'S HEADQUARTERS.
WE DON'T KNOW HOW IT HAPPENED, BUT THE BOY DEFINITELY HAS DEFENDER'S POWERS.
THOUGH NOT HIS SKILLS OR STRENGTH . . . YET.

THEIR ENERGY IMPRINTS ARE AN EXACT MATCH, SIR.

PITY HE WON'T LIVE LONG ENOUGH TO DEVELOP THOSE SKILLS!

IF WE MEASURE THE FORCE OF DEFENDER'S BLOWS BY POUNDS PER SQUARE INCH, OR PSI . . .
SINCE FORCE IS EQUAL TO MASS TIMES ACCELERATION, AND ONE POUND IS ROUGHLY EQUAL TO 4.5 NEWTONS—

IN ENGLISH, PLEASE
DEFENDER'S PUNCHES INITIALLY CLOCKED IN AT 600 PSI. BY THE TIME HE MET HIS DEMISE, THAT NUMBER HAD GONE UP TO 1,000 PSI.

IF DEFENDER'S POWERS INCREASED OVER TIME, IT STANDS TO REASON THAT SMASH'S WILL, AS WELL.

ESPECIALLY SINCE SMASH HASN'T EVEN GONE THROUGH PUBERTY! HE COULD END UP AT 1,000 PSI . . .
OR EVEN 2,000! WE JUST DON'T KNOW. THE MIND BOGGLES!

THEN, IF I WAIT TO TAKE HIS POWERS . . .
THERE COULD BE MORE POWERS TO TAKE!
SINCE WE DON'T UNDERSTAND THESE POWERS, THERE'S NO WAY TO BE CERTAIN.

IN THE MEANTIME, SMASH MAY GROW STRONGER . . . BETTER . . . AND MORE DIFFICULT TO CATCH.
WELL, OF COURSE, THAT'S POSSIBLE . . .

GREED HAS BEEN MY UNDOING FAR TOO OFTEN.

I'D RATHER TAKE HIS POWERS NOW THAN WAIT UNTIL HE'S UNSTOPPABLE.

A WISE CHOICE, WISE ONE! YOUR WISDOM IS INCALCULABLE!
WE'RE STILL ALIVE! I CAN'T EVEN BELIEVE IT!

THE RYANS' HOUSE.
HOW DOES IT FEEL TO BE THE **FIRST** CRIMINAL APPREHENDED BY **SMASH?**

WHEN I GET OUTTA HERE, I'LL **SHOW** THAT SNOT-NOSED BRAT—

NO COMMENT!
MY CLIENT IS **INNOCENT!** SHUT THAT THING **OFF!**

FASCINATING. WHEN WE COME BACK . . .

ARE YOU BOTH PACKED? YOUR **FATHER'S** HERE, SO GET YOUR BAGS.

I'M **NOT** GOING TO DAD'S **STUPID** APARTMENT!

IT'S HIS WEEKEND TO SEE YOU, TOMMY. GET **BACK** HERE!

I DON'T CARE! THERE'S A PARTY TOMORROW NIGHT AND I'M **NOT** MISSING IT TO HANG OUT WITH **DAD!**
AND MY NAME'S **TOM,** NOT TOMMY! I'M NOT A BABY ANYMORE!

HEY, BIG GUY! HOW 'BOUT A HUG?

DROP DEAD.

I DON'T KNOW WHAT'S GOTTEN INTO TOMMY LATELY!
HE'S A TEENAGER, THAT'S ALL.
HIYA, DAD!

I PACKED MY COSTUME, IN CASE I CAN SNEAK AWAY TO USE IT. TOO BAD DAD DOESN'T WORK NIGHTS LIKE MOM DOES!
WHO WANTS ICE CREAM?

SOUNDS GREAT!

HOW'S SCHOOL?
GOOD.
HOW'S YOUR MOM?
GOOD.
HOW'S YOUR ICE CREAM?
GOOD.
RING!
RING!

WHAT'S GOING ON?
WE NEED BACKUP, RIGHT NOW!
HELLO? I CAN'T TALK NOW, MY KID IS—WHAT? I NEVER SAID THAT!

WHAT THE—?
WELL, WHO SAID I SAID IT? HE SAID IT OR YOU SAID IT?
FOOM!

SWEET, SASSY CRAP!
I KNOW YOU JUST SAID IT! BUT WHO SAID IT BEFORE YOU SAID IT?
BOOM!

LOOK OUT!
I DON'T THINK HE SAID WHAT YOU'RE SAYING HE SAID! WAIT— WHAT ARE YOU SAYING?

KEEE-RASH!!!
DAD, ARE YOU OK? SAY SOMETHING! DAD?!

GET OUTTA THE WAY!
WOO! WOO! WOO!

THIS IS DETECTIVE DOUROUX! WE'VE GOT A HELICOPTER DOWN AND SHOTS FIRED! I NEED SOME SERIOUS BACKUP! ALL UNITS—

OH, MAN . . .

THIS AIN'T HAPPENING!

MY CAAAAAAAAAAAR!

THE ICE-CREAM PARLOR.
C'MON, DAD, YOU'VE GOTTA BE OK! CAN YOU HEAR ME? SAY SOMETHING!

OVER HERE! MAN DOWN!

PLEASE, GIVE US SOME ROOM! IS THAT YOUR FATHER?
Y-YEAH . . . IS HE GONNA LIVE?
I'VE GOT A PULSE!

LISTEN TO ME. WE'RE TAKING YOUR DAD TO THE HOSPITAL. WE'LL TAKE CARE OF HIM—I PROMISE!
EVEN WITH ALL MY NEW POWERS, I COULDN'T PROTECT MY OWN DAD!

WHERE'D THAT KID GO?

BUT I CAN MAKE WHOEVER DID THIS SORRY HE WAS EVER BORN!

EAGLE ONE TO NEST! I'M IN POSITION!
HAVE YOU GOT HIM IN YOUR SIGHTS?

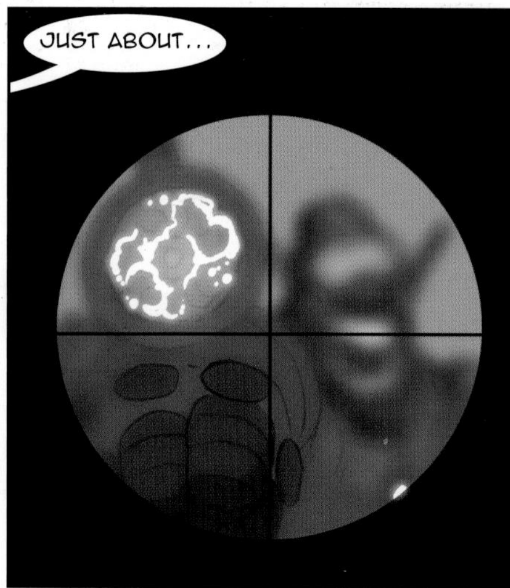
JUST ABOUT...

THERE HE IS!

WUH-OH!

FOOM!

WHO ELSE WANTS A TASTE? C'MON, COPS, IS THAT ALL YOU GOT?

WHAT'S THE SITUATION, OFFICER?
SOME NUT JOB CALLING HIMSELF "PULSE" HIJACKED AN ARMORED CAR DURING RUSH HOUR! THEN HE STARTED BLASTING AT EVERYTHING!
DON'T WORRY, THERE'S MORE BACKUP ON THE WAY!

EVERY TIME MORE BACKUP ARRIVES, HE JUST TRASHES IT!
DON'T LOOK NOW, ROOKIE . . .

BUT HERE COMES THE CAVALRY!

THIS IS THE POLICE! YOU GOT ONE CHANCE—DROP YOUR WEAPONS NOW!
THIS IS MORE LIKE IT! HIT ME WITH YOUR BEST SHOT, COPS!

FOOM!!

GAME OVER, SUCKERS!
PTUI!

I'M GOIN' HOME—AND I'M TAKIN' MY TOYS WITH ME.

YA KNOW, ON SECOND THOUGHT . . .

I GOT TIME FOR ONE MORE ROUND!

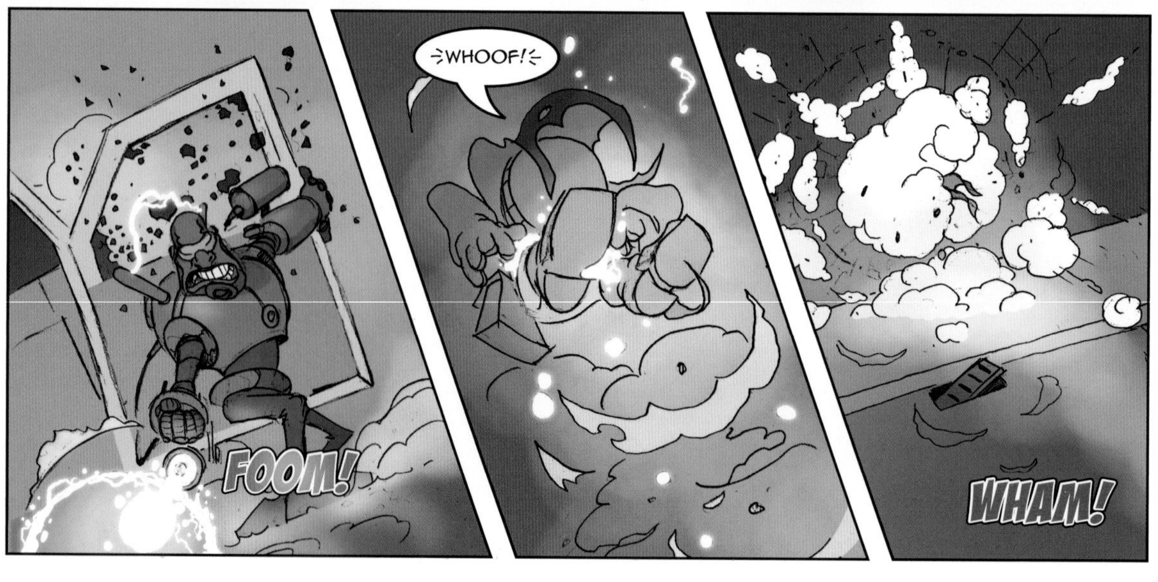
FOOM!
WHOOF!
WHAM!

HIT HIM WITH EVERYTHING BEFORE HE GETS AWAY! NOW!

BLAM! BLAM!
PUM! PUM! PUM!
BUDABUDABUDA!

THOSE LITTLE PIGGIES DON'T GET NO ROAST BEEF!

HIT THE GAS, SON!

WE'RE GOIN' WEE, WEE, WEE, ALL THE WAY HOME!
SCREEEEEECH!

AIM FOR THE TIRES!
PUM! PUM!

WHAT THE—?
HEY! LOOK OUT!
THAT'S SMASH?
HE REALLY IS A KID!
PARDON ME! 'SCUSE ME! SORRY—COMING THROUGH!

WOOOOO-WEE! THE COPS CAN'T STOP ME . . . THE SUPER-KID CAN'T STOP ME . . .
I'M UNSTOPPABLE!

DON'T STOP FOR ANY RED LIGHTS, BUDDY!
GOTTA SNEAK IN LOW SO HE DOESN'T SPOT ME. . . .

A LITTLE CLOSER, NOW . . . ALMOST THERE . . .

HUH? WELL, LOOKIT THAT!

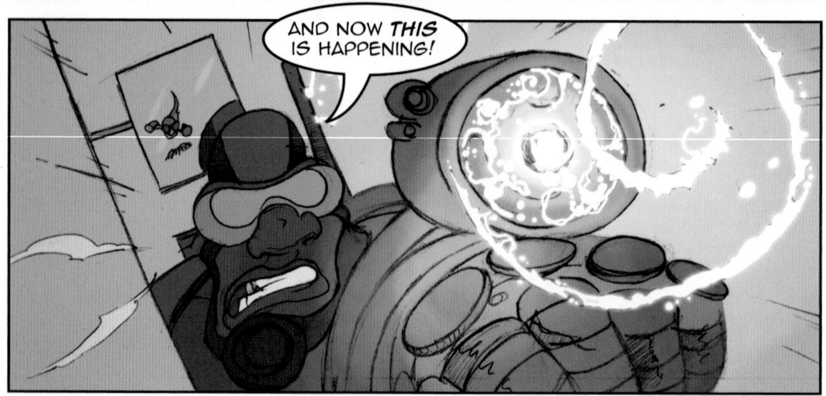
AND NOW THIS IS HAPPENING!

HERE COMES THE PAIN, KID!

WHOOPS! OH, THIS ISN'T GOOD!

YIKES! THAT WAS TOO CLOSE!
FOOM!

STOP, YOU MANIAC! YOU'RE GONNA HURT INNOCENT PEOPLE!
THAT INCLUDES YOU, IF YOU DON'T KEEP THAT PEDAL TO THE FLOOR! GOT ME?

LET'S TRY THAT AGAIN . . . A LITTLE MORE CAREFULLY THIS TIME!

IF I USE THIS BUS FOR COVER, HE WON'T SEE ME UNTIL IT'S TOO LATE!
I KNOW YOU'RE HERE SOMEWHERE, KID! COME OUT, COME OUT, WHEREVER YOU ARE!

IT'S SMASH!
HE'S REAL!
QUIT PUSHING!
IS HE CUTE?
LET ME SEE!

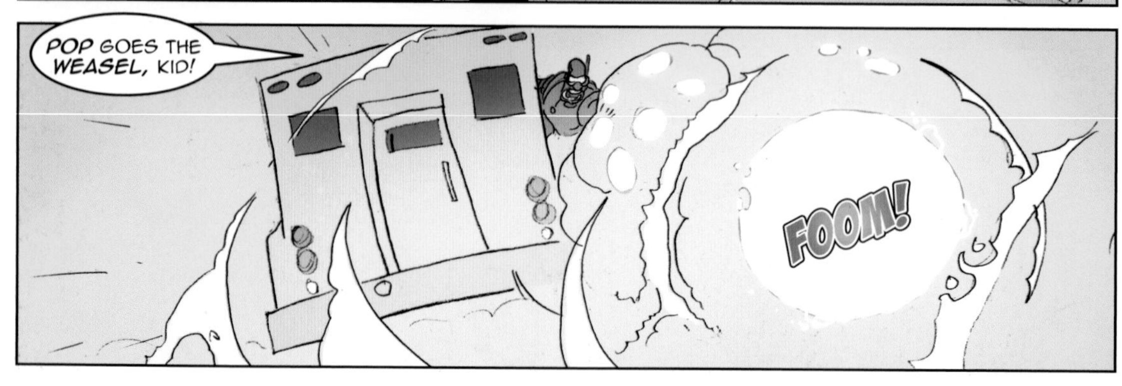
POP GOES THE WEASEL, KID!
FOOM!

BA-DOOM!!
NO!

AAAAIIIIEEEEE! WE'RE ALL GOING TO DIE!
I DON'T THINK I'M STRONG ENOUGH TO CATCH A BUS . . . BUT I'VE GOTTA TRY!
PLEASE DON'T LET THIS HURT TOO MUCH! OR KILL ME TOO MUCH!

OOF! GOT IT!

SCREEEEEEEEEE!
UH, MAYBE NOT!

HELP! HELP US! SOMEBODY HELLLLPP!

SCREEEEEEEEEEEEEEEEECH!!

IS EVERYONE ALIVE? TELL ME YOU'RE ALL OK!
I'M DIZZY!

C'MON, GIRLS— ONE AT A TIME! LET'S ALL TRY TO CALM DOWN . . .
WHAT ABOUT SMASH? DID HE SURVIVE?

HERE HE IS, OVER HERE!
WOW . . .

AHEM! HI, GIRLS. HOW Y'ALL DOIN' TODAY?
CAN ONE OF YOU OPEN THIS WINDOW?

DID YOU SEE THAT? WHAT A FLIP!
YOU'RE REALLY NUTS, YOU KNOW THAT?!

GOTTA STOP THAT GUY BEFORE ANYONE ELSE GETS HURT!
HEY, NOW! TALK NICE TO THE CRAZY GUY HOLDING AN ELECTROMAGNETIC BLASTER TO YOUR SKULL!

YOU GOTTA BE KIDDIN' ME . . .

THE KID IS BACK?!

FOOM!
SON, I GIVE YA PROPS FOR TRYIN'!

CRIMINY SAKES, THAT WAS CLOSE!
FOOM!

MAYBE I CAN GET TO HIM THROUGH THE BACK! I HOPE IT'S UNLOCKED . . .
YOU WANT A LITTLE MORE? I CAN DO THIS ALL WEEKEND AND INTO NEXT WEEK!

BETTER BUCKLE UP . . .
CLICK!

SCREEEEEEEEEEEEECH!!
GUHH!
WHUMP!

OH, NO!
I'VE GOTTA GET SOME BRAKES!

WHUNK!
WHAT HIT US?

CRASH!!

LOOK OUT!
SKRIIIIIIIICH!!

WHOA, THE WHOLE WORLD'S SPINNING . . .
THUNK!

JOHN WOO JUMP!

FOOM!
FOOM!
FOOM!
MANGA SLIDE!

THERE'S MY LITTLE MAN! I GOT SOMETHIN' SPECIAL FOR YA!

I DON'T THINK I'M GONNA GET ANOTHER CHANCE . . .

OH, PLEASE LET THIS WORK!

WHOOSH!

NOW I WISH I'D PLAYED BASEBALL!
NONONONONO . . .

NO! NOT THE MONEY!
KRESH!

THAT DOES IT! I'M THROUGH PLAYIN'!
FFFFFFFFFFFOOOOO...

OH, MAN! I SHOULD'A GOT THE WARRANTY!
ZZZZZZZZTT!

THUNK!

YESSSS! GOT IT IN ONE!

ALL RIGHT, NOBODY MOVE!
HEY FELLAS, NO WORRIES!
THE CREEP'S ALL TAKEN CARE OF. NO ONE NEEDS TO THANK ME, JUST DOING MY DUTY—

HANDCUFF THIS KID! SMASH, YOU'RE UNDER ARREST!

HUH? ARE YOU JOKING? WHAT FOR?

RECKLESS ENDANGERMENT, DESTRUCTION OF PROPERTY... I CAN'T EVEN COUNT ALL THE LAWS YOU BROKE!
NOT TO MENTION YOU COULD'VE KILLED SOMEBODY!
NEXT TIME A SIMPLE "THANKS" WILL DO!

GEEZ, THAT COP WAS SUCH A JERK!

BET NOBODY TRIED TO ARREST **DEFENDER** FOR BEING A HERO!

DAD'S GOTTA BE AROUND HERE **SOMEWHERE.**

ACT LIKE YOU **KNOW** WHERE YOU'RE GOING . . . NO ONE WILL **NOTICE** YOU . . .

I'VE GOT K-9 UNITS **AND** PATROL CARS SCOURING THE AREA. DON'T WORRY, WE'LL FIND—
MOM? DAD?

ANDREW?
THERE HE IS! I TOLD YOU HE'D TURN UP!

WE WERE SO WORRIED—NO ONE COULD FIND YOU! ARE YOU HURT?
I'M FINE! I GOT SCARED AND HID UNTIL THE COAST WAS CLEAR.

H-HOW ARE YOU, DAD? ARE YOU HURT REALLY BAD?
I GOT A FEW DINGS, BUT IT LOOKS WORSE THAN IT IS. I'LL BE BACK ON MY FEET IN NO TIME!
I'M JUST GLAD YOU'RE ALL RIGHT.

I HATE TO INTERRUPT, BUT I NEED TO TAKE CARE OF SOME BUSINESS.
ANDREW, I'M DETECTIVE DOUROUX OF THE SEATOWN POLICE DEPARTMENT.

AM—AM I UNDER ARREST?

DON'T BE SILLY, HONEY! WHAT WOULD MAKE YOU THINK THAT?
I JUST NEED TO ASK A FEW QUESTIONS ABOUT WHAT YOU SAW TODAY.

HOSPITAL CAFETERIA.
AND FROM WHERE YOU WERE HIDING, YOU COULDN'T SEE ANYTHING ELSE?
NOPE—I HAD MY EYES COVERED MOST OF THE TIME. SORRY...

NO NEED TO APOLOGIZE, ANDREW. YOU'VE BEEN VERY HELPFUL. WE'LL CATCH THIS "SMASH" CHARACTER ONE WAY OR ANOTHER!
HE DOESN'T SEEM LIKE A BAD GUY! AND I THINK HIS REAL NAME IS SPARROW—
DO YOU REALLY THINK SMASH IS A LITTLE KID?

DON'T SEE HOW HE COULD BE. IT'S PROBABLY ANOTHER TRICK CREATED BY THE MAGUS. IF YOU THINK OF ANYTHING ELSE, GIVE ME A CALL.

WHEW! THAT WAS CLOSE. I THOUGHT HE FIGURED ME OUT FOR SURE!
I HAVE TO GO BACK TO WORK, ANDREW. DO YOU FEEL OK TAKING THE BUS HOME?

A SHORT WHILE LATER.
GUESS THERE'S NO USE FIGHTING IT. EVERYONE'S CALLING ME SMASH, WHETHER I LIKE IT OR NOT!
WHUP! WHUP! WHUP!

WHUP!
WHUP!
WHUP!
HOLD IT RIGHT THERE, SMASH!
NOT AGAIN! CAN'T YOU COPS GIVE IT A REST?!

EASY, KID! YOU'RE NOT IN DANGER!
I HAD AN ARRANGEMENT WITH DEFENDER THAT I COULD CONTACT HIM WHENEVER THERE'S **TROUBLE.**

TAKE THIS— IT'S A **SPECIAL** PHONE.
CAN WE CALL **YOU** NOW WHEN WE NEED HELP?

COOL! IT'S NOT EXACTLY THE BAT SIGNAL . . . BUT IT'LL WORK!

THANKS, CAPTAIN RAMSEY!
SEE YA AROUND!

YEAH . . . SEE YOU.

WHUP! WHUP! WHUP! WHUP!

I SHOULD STUDY FOR THAT TEST ON MONDAY, BUT I'M BEAT! STILL . . . IF I DON'T PASS, I'LL BE GROUNDED!
FOUND YOU . . .

MONDAY MORNING.
UGH. FEELS LIKE I SLEPT THE WHOLE WEEKEND! AND I'M STILL TIRED!
AND I NEVER DID STUDY! BETTER CRAM DURING RECESS . . .

EXCUSE ME, YOUNG MAN . . .
CAN I HELP YOU?

I JUST WANTED TO SEE WHAT SMASH REALLY LOOKS LIKE!

I, UM . . . **WHO'S** SMASH? I DON'T . . .

WHAT'S WRONG, **SMASH?** NEVER HAD SOMEBODY GUESS YOUR **SECRET IDENTITY** BEFORE?
I'VE BEEN WATCHING YOU SINCE—

CRUNCH!
GAAAAAHHH!

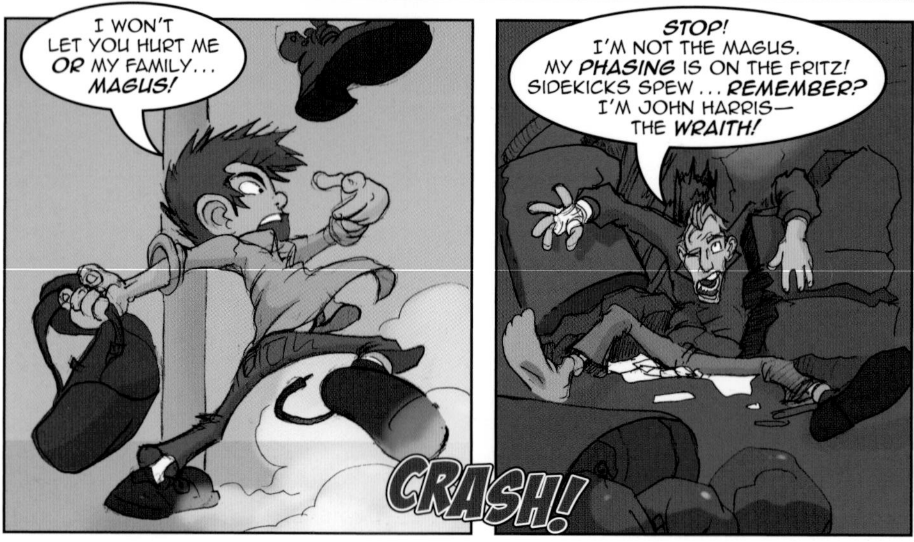
I WON'T LET YOU HURT ME **OR** MY FAMILY . . . **MAGUS!**
STOP! I'M NOT THE MAGUS. MY **PHASING** IS ON THE FRITZ! SIDEKICKS SPEW . . . **REMEMBER?** I'M JOHN HARRIS— THE **WRAITH!**
CRASH!

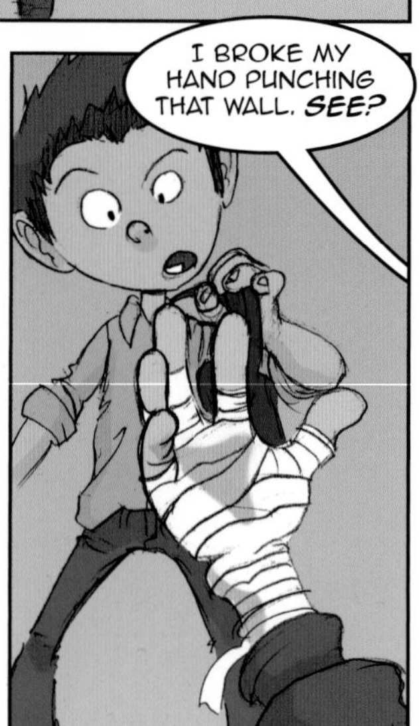
I BROKE MY HAND PUNCHING THAT WALL. **SEE?**

WHAT'S THE BIG IDEA, SCARING ME LIKE THAT?! HOW DID YOU FIND ME?
FIRST RULE OF BEING A HERO: IF YOU WANT YOUR SECRET IDENTITY TO **STAY** SECRET, **DON'T** FLY HOME WEARING YOUR **COSTUME!**

YOU WERE SO **EASY** TO FOLLOW—
WHAT, ARE YOU **STALKING** ME NOW?

YOU NEED TRAINING! HERE'S MY CARD—
I DON'T WANT YOUR STUPID CARD! TRAIN **YOURSELF** TO STOP BEING A **CREEP!**

I'M GONNA BE LATE FOR SCHOOL.
TAKE THE CARD ANYWAY— JUST IN CASE!

LEAVE ME ALONE, MISTER STRANGER! I DON'T **WANNA** RIDE IN YOUR **VAN!**

HEH, HEH . . . HE WAS KIDDING. REALLY! WE'RE OLD **FRIENDS.**

ELSEWHERE.
DR. COBB HAS EXCEEDED MY EXPECTATIONS.

I'M PLEASED HE FINISHED EARLY. THE QUESTION IS, DOES IT *WORK?*

IT ALL *SEEMS* FUNCTIONAL . . . THOUGH, OF COURSE, WE HAVE NO WAY TO *TEST* IT.

NOT TRUE. THE DEVICE IS ABOUT TO HAVE ITS ONE AND *ONLY* TEST.

POLICE HEADQUARTERS.
BZZT! BZZT!
NOW WHAT?

RAMSEY HERE.
DO YOU RECOGNIZE MY VOICE?

THE TIME HAS COME TO *BAIT* THE *TRAP.* DO IT NOW.

AT SCHOOL.
WISH I'D STUDIED THIS WEEKEND!
STUPID PULSE AND HIS STUPID ROBBERY!

WHUNG!
WHAT THE . . . ?

NICE REFLEXES, BOOKWORM!
WHAT'S THE MATTER? MOMMY WON'T LET YOU PLAY WITH OTHER KIDS?

HEARD YOUR DAD GOT BEAT UP BY THAT LAME PULSE GUY. GUESS YOUR WHOLE FAMILY'S A BUNCH OF WIMPS!

THAT DOES IT! YOU WANT A FIGHT, GARETH? YOU'RE GONNA GET—

UH . . . 'SCUSE ME A SEC!
BZZT!
BZZT!

H-HELLO? UH, I MEAN, ⇒AHEM!⇐ SMASH SPEAKING!

WE'VE CORNERED A MINION INSIDE THE OLD FIREHOUSE ON FIFTH AND MAIN.

NOW? CAN IT WAIT TILL THREE?

CRIME DOESN'T HAPPEN ON YOUR SCHEDULE! IF YOU WANNA TAKE OVER FOR DEFENDER—
OK, OK! I'M ON MY WAY!

I'LL THINK UP AN EXCUSE LATER. RIGHT NOW I NEED A DIVERSION....

IT'S MINE, GARETH! GIVE IT BACK!
ALL YOU GOTTA DO IS TAKE IT, SHRIMP!

KUNG!

AWESOME SHOT!
GARETH! SPEAK TO ME!

THERE'S FIFTH, BUT WHERE'S MAIN? I CAN'T FIND IT ANYWHERE!
WHO MADE THIS DUMB MAP?

THERE'S THE GPS SIGNAL FROM THE PHONE!
HE'S FLYING IN CIRCLES. THINK HE FIGURED US OUT?
IF SO, HE'S FAR SMARTER THAN I'D EVER IMAGINED.

NO WONDER! IT WAS UPSIDE DOWN! GOTTA GO EAST...
WHICH WAY IS EAST?

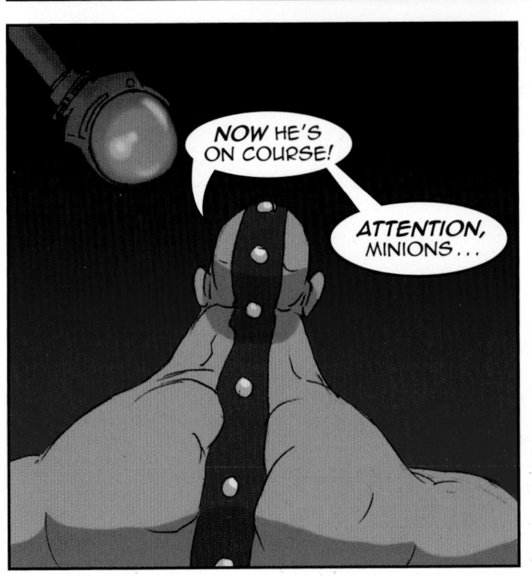
NOW HE'S ON COURSE!
ATTENTION, MINIONS...

THAT'S THE FIREHOUSE, BUT WHERE ARE ALL THE COPS?
THE MOSQUITO IS IN THE NET....

SWAT IT!

POOM!
POOM!

NETS? IT'S A TRAP!

WHEW! SOMETIMES IT PAYS TO BE SMALL!

BLAZES! THE NETS WERE DESIGNED FOR DEFENDER! THEY'RE TOO BIG FOR THAT LITTLE PIMPLE!
UH, WHOOPS . . .

SECOND WAVE, GO!
YES, SIR!

OUR TURN!

YAAAAA!
IT'S RAINING MINIONS?!

HA! MISSED ME, YOU CRAZY—

WHUNF!

GOTTA SCRAPE HIM OFF!

CLANG!
AT LEAST THE MINIONS ARE TOO BIG TO LAND ON ONE OF THESE. . . .

OH, NO!

CRUNCH!
STUPID, STUPID MINION!

THEY'RE EVERYWHERE, I CAN'T SHAKE 'EM! GOTTA GET OUT OF HERE....

WHY DO I ALWAYS GET STUCK WAITING? I NEVER GET A CHANCE TO—

AHA!
LET GO OF ME!

HERE WE GO AGAIN...

I'VE HAD ENOUGH OF THIS!

CRACK!
HAVE A NICE TRIP, FELLAS! SEE YOU IN THE FALL!

LOOKS LIKE THEY'RE ALL OUT OF MINIONS!

WHAP!
UNGH!

HEY! WHERE'D YOU COME FROM?

SPLOOSH!

NOW WHERE'D HE GO?
FZZZZT

THIRD WAVE TO BASE. THE BUG IS ZAPPED.

WAKEY, WAKEY, SMASH!

MUCH BETTER.

HEROES DON'T GET NAP TIMES, YOUNG MAN!

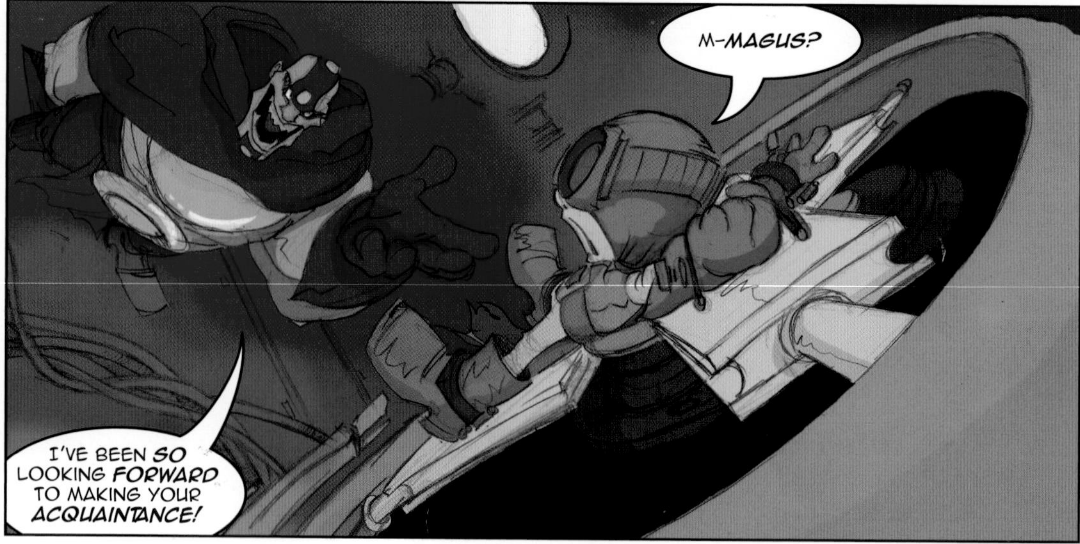
M-MAGUS?
I'VE BEEN SO LOOKING FORWARD TO MAKING YOUR ACQUAINTANCE!

LATER.
WELL? IS IT SMASH?
CAN'T TELL YET. IT LOOKS LIKE PART OF HIS COSTUME. I'LL COMPARE IT TO THE SAMPLES FROM THE BANK ROBBERY, BUT IT'LL TAKE A FEW HOURS TO GET RESULTS.
WE DON'T HAVE A FEW HOURS!

THE LADY IN THREE-A SAW SMASH GET "ZAPPED"— HER WORD—BY SOME KIND OF ELECTRICAL DEVICE. NOBODY SAW IF HE FLEW AWAY OR GOT CARRIED OFF.

HEY, OVER HERE! I FOUND SOME—

THWACK!!

BACK OFF!

HOLD IT RIGHT THERE!
WHAP!

CHOK!

YAAAAAAAAHHHH!

YOU GOT THE RIGHT TO REMAIN SILENT!
THWUMP!

BUT, FOR YOUR OWN SAFETY...
HUHHK! HUUUHHKK!

I SUGGEST YOU DON'T USE IT!

THE OLD FIREHOUSE.
AT LAST WE MEET! THE PLEASURE'S ALL MINE, I'M SURE.
MAKE THIS EASY ON YOURSELF, MAGUS. GIVE UP WITHOUT A F-F-FIGHT.

HA! HA! PRECIOUS CHILD! I'M SURE YOUR TEACHERS ARE DELIGHTED BY YOUR IMAGINATION!
NOT REALLY . . .

NOR AM I. YOU HAVE WHAT'S RIGHTFULLY MINE. I DON'T KNOW HOW YOU GOT DEFENDER'S POWERS, BUT THEY BELONG TO ME—AND I INTEND TO TAKE THEM!

DON'T WORRY—I BEAR YOU NO GRUDGE. ONCE I'VE DRAINED YOUR POWERS, I'LL LET YOU LEAVE UNHARMED.
ASSUMING YOU SURVIVE THE TRANSFERENCE PROCESS!

WHAT DO YOU WANT THESE POWERS FOR? WHY DON'T YOU JUST MAKE SOME FOR YOURSELF?
IF THE PROCESS COULD BE REPLICATED, I WOULD. BUT IT WAS AN ACCIDENT THAT CREATED THOSE POWERS—AND DECEIT THAT STOLE THEM FROM ME!
WHAT ARE YOU TALKING ABOUT?

"MANY YEARS AGO, I WAS ONE OF A DOZEN TEST SUBJECTS IN AN EXPERIMENT TO EXPAND THE BOUNDARIES OF HUMAN ENDURANCE. I TRAINED RIGOROUSLY—OBSESSIVELY—TO BECOME THE TOP CANDIDATE IN THE PROGRAM."

"SADLY, MY MOMENT OF GLORY WAS STOLEN BY MY CLOSEST COMPETITOR! I COULDN'T PROVE IT, BUT I KNOW HE CHEATED TO WIN THE TOP SPOT!"

"DURING THE EXPERIMENT, THE MACHINE SOMEHOW MALFUNCTIONED. THE EXPLOSION BOMBARDED HIM WITH ENERGY THAT GAVE HIM SUPERHUMAN STRENGTH AND THE ABILITY TO FLY."

"YES, THAT'S RIGHT . . . HE BECAME DEFENDER! USING POWERS THAT SHOULD HAVE BEEN MINE!"
"WHEN THE LAB WAS REBUILT, I FINALLY HAD MY CHANCE! HOWEVER, NO MATTER HOW HARD THEY TRIED, THE SCIENTISTS COULD NEVER DUPLICATE THE ACCIDENT."

"WHILE MY SIZE AND STRENGTH WERE INCREASED BEYOND THAT OF A NORMAL HUMAN, THEY'RE NOTHING COMPARED TO DEFENDER'S ABILITIES!"

BUT NOW, AT LONG LAST, I SHALL CLAIM WHAT WAS RIGHTFULLY MINE!
I ASSURE YOU, THIS WILL GO MUCH EASIER IF YOU DON'T RESIST. THAT'S WHAT COST DEFENDER HIS LIFE!

I'M DOOMED! IF DEFENDER COULDN'T SURVIVE THE MAGUS'S MACHINE, WHAT CHANCE DO I HAVE?!

SHOULD'A LISTENED TO WRAITH . . . EVEN IF HE IS A WEIRDO! I'M NO HERO, I'M JUST A KID!

HRRRRK!

IT'S NO USE! I'M NOT STRONG ENOUGH.

GOTTA FACE FACTS. THERE'S NO WAY I—

THIS IS PROMISING. . . .

POLICE HEADQUARTERS.
RIGHT NOW YOU'RE LOOKIN' AT A LIFETIME IN PRISON! BUT IF YOU TELL US WHERE MAGUS IS HOLDING SMASH, I'LL TALK TO THE DA ABOUT A DEAL—
UH, DETECTIVE DOUROUX?

IT'S BEEN AN HOUR AND HE HASN'T SAID SQUAT! I DON'T THINK HE'S GONNA TALK.
MAYBE I'M ASKING THE WRONG GUY.

CAPTAIN RAMSEY!
SPLURK!

IF YOU'VE GOT A MAN ON THE INSIDE, CALL HIM—NOW—AND FIND OUT WHERE THE MAGUS IS!

FIRST OFF, I DON'T ANSWER TO YOU! AND SECOND—
SAVE IT! A BOY'S LIFE IS AT STAKE! WE'VE GOTTA MOVE NOW!

GET OUT OF MY OFFICE WHILE YOU STILL HAVE A BADGE.

IF ANYTHING HAPPENS TO THAT KID, I'M HOLDING YOU RESPONSIBLE . . . CAPTAIN!

THE OLD FIREHOUSE.
ONLY TWO MINIONS! BETTER MAKE MY MOVE BEFORE **OTHERS** SHOW UP!
INITIATE ***PRE-ACTIVATION*** SEQUENCE!

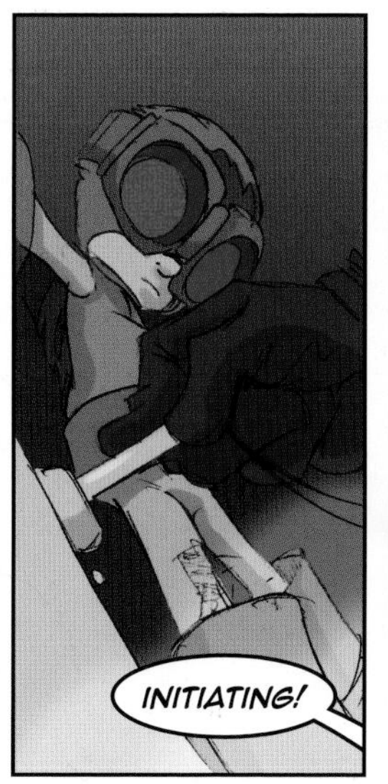
INITIATING!

EVERYONE HAS THOSE ***KEYS*** AROUND THEIR NECKS!

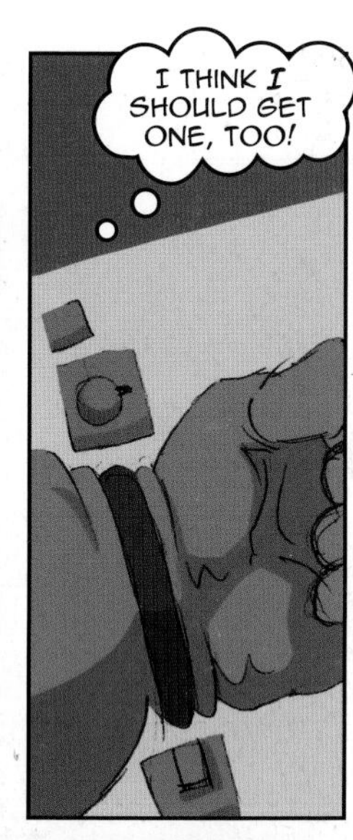
I THINK ***I*** SHOULD GET ONE, TOO!

NICE AND ***SLOW.*** ***EASY*** DOES IT . . .

ALMOOOOST GOT IIIIIIIIIIIIT. . .

WHAT THE?

WHAP!

OH, I'M SO GONNA GET BLAMED FOR THIS!

C'MON, C'MON! GET A GRIP!

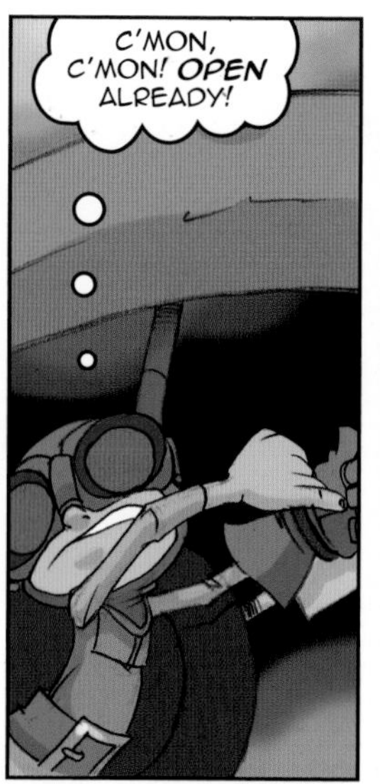
C'MON, C'MON! OPEN ALREADY!

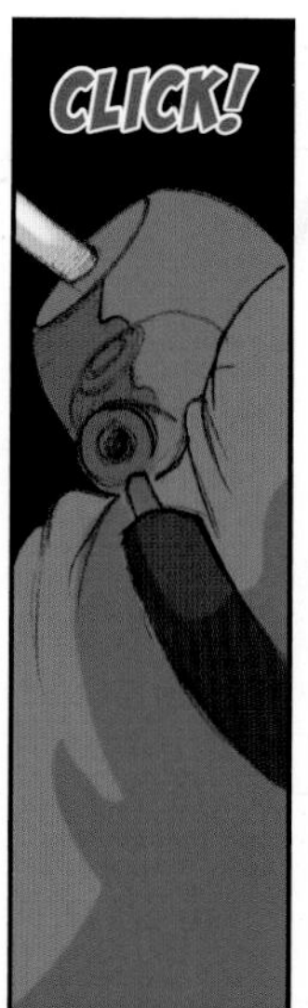
CLICK!

HERE WE GO....

GOT IT!
HAVE YOU FINISHED THE INITIATION PROCEDURE?
UH-OH...

SSSSSSTTTTT!

ARE WE READY FOR THE, UH...?

SUFFERING QUARKS!
THUD!

PLEASE HIT SOMETHING!
KUNG!

CRASH!!

ALMOST FREE!

HE'S ALMOST FREE! PUSH THE BUTTON!

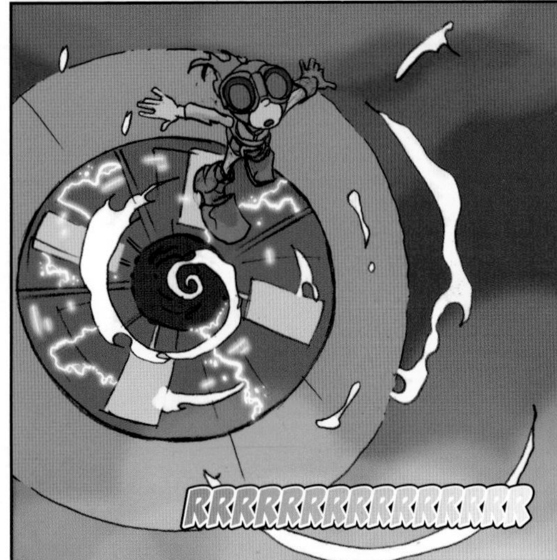

RRRRRRRRRRRRRRRRR

GAAAAHHH!
FOOOOOOOM!

BOOM!
KERR-
ESH!

THE PROCEDURE WAS INTERRUPTED! QUICK, ALERT THE MAGUS—
THAT SMARTED!

HOLY MAMA!

FWUMP!

WHOOSH!

I FEEL SO WEIRD, LIKE I'M NOT ALL HERE! WHAT'D THEY DO TO ME?
GOTTA PULL MYSELF TOGETHER AND GET MOVING BEFORE . . .

AHHH . . . YOU DON'T DISAPPOINT ME, LITTLE ONE!

I ADMIRE YOUR PERSISTENCE AND ***PLUCK.***

BUT YOU CAN'T ESCAPE.

YOU SEE, THE ***ONLY*** WAY OUT . . .

IS ***THROUGH ME!***
OK, JUST THINK: WHAT WOULD ***DEFENDER*** DO?

GRAAAHHH!

HERE GOES NOTHING!

GRAAAAAAAH!

YAAAAAAAH!

MADE IT THROUGH!

I SURE HOPE HE'S NOT AS **FAST** AS ME!

BETTER LUCK NEXT TIME, MAGUS!

WHICH WAY LEADS **OUT** OF HERE?

ULP! NOT **THAT** WAY!

HOW'D **HE** GET LOOSE?
I KNEW I SHOULD'VE TAKEN THAT **LEFT** TURN!

WHO CARES? GRAB HIM!

POW!

WHAP!

LET'S TRY THE OTHER WAY!

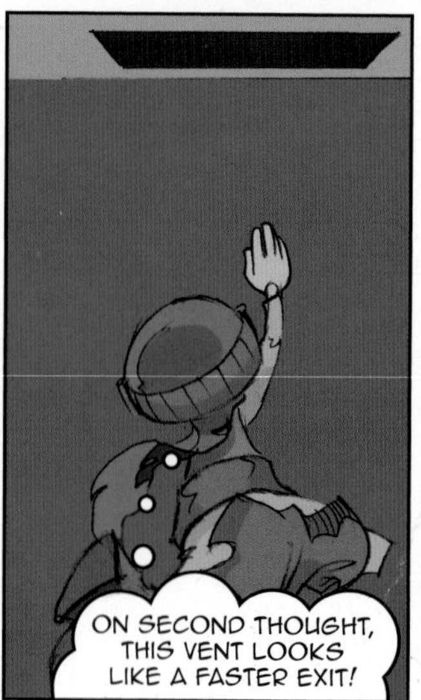
ON SECOND THOUGHT, THIS VENT LOOKS LIKE A FASTER EXIT!

UNGH! WHAT THE?

PLAYTIME'S OVER, BOY!
WHUMP!

EITHER HE'S **STRONGER** THAN I THOUGHT, OR I'VE GOTTEN A LOT **WEAKER!**

I AM **NOT** AMUSED!
HUUKK! YEAH, I CAN SEE THAT!

IT OCCURS TO ME I DON'T NEED YOU **ALIVE** TO DRAIN YOUR POWERS!

CAN'T GO **RIGH**T . . . CAN'T GO **LEFT** . . . CAN'T REACH THE **VENT!** LOOKS LIKE THE **ONLY** WAY OUT IS . . .
UP.

YOU **WANT** THESE POWERS, MAGUS?
HURK! LET'S SEE HOW **BAD!**

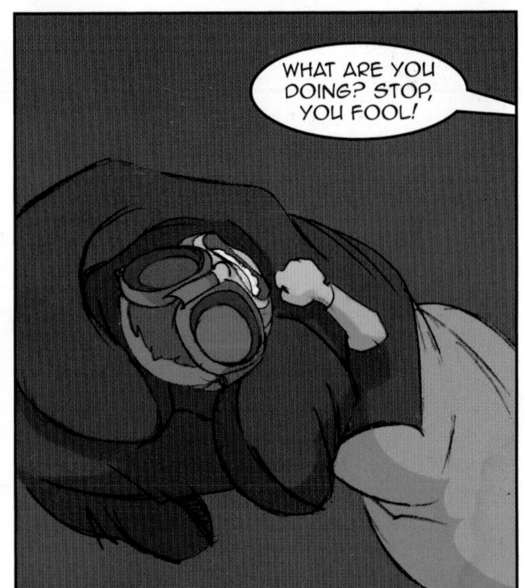
WHAT ARE YOU DOING? STOP, YOU FOOL!

IF SMASH MAKES IT OUT OF THIS BUILDING ALIVE . . .
CRUNCH!

CRASH!
I SWEAR, BY ALL THE POWER AT MY DISPOSAL . . .

QUICKLY, ALERT THE GUARDS!

HOW MANY FLOORS DOES THIS PLACE HAVE?
HOPE THIS IS THE ROOF. . . .

FINALLY GET A FEW MINUTES TO MYSELF . . . BEST PART OF MY DAY!

GAH! OCCUPIED!!
SORRY— DIDN'T SEE A THING!

OPEN AIR— I MADE IT OUT!
WHUD!
YOU'RE ALL FIRED!
CRASH!
WHAM!

GIVE UP YET?
SHOOT HIM, YOU FOOLS!
I CAN'T GET A CLEAN SHOT! I'LL HIT THE MAGUS!

FEEL SO . . . WOOZY . . . CAN'T GO MUCH FARTHER! GOTTA . . . SCRAPE HIM . . . OFF!

GASP!
THERE!
HUNFF!
CRUNCH!

SO TIRED . . . BLACKING OUT . . . I'M A GONER!

GOTTA AIM FOR . . . THE WATER . . . SOFT LANDING . . .

SPLOOSH!

LATER.
SIR, THE TUNNELS ARE *EMPTY!* THE DIVERS HAVEN'T FOUND A BODY . . .

KEEP LOOKING. WE'LL SCOUR THE OCEAN FLOOR, IF NECESSARY! WHATEVER IT TAKES . . . WE *WILL* FIND THAT *BOY!*

MEANWHILE . . .

WITNESSES REPORTED SEEING THE MAGUS STRUGGLING WITH A FIGURE WHO APPEARED TO BE *SMASH* . . .
CAUSING INCREDIBLE DAMAGE TO THE FIREHOUSE.

DING-DONG!
WHO JUST *DROPS BY* THIS LATE?

IF IT'S AN OLD VILLAIN LOOKING TO SETTLE SOME SCORE, HE'S IN FOR A *REAL*—

SMASH?
TRAIN ME . . .